Betwixt Mountain and Wilderness

TIMOTHY WANGUSA

Nsemia

First Edition: June 2015
Published by Nsemia Inc. Publishers (www.nsemia.com); Oakville, Ontario, Canada

Edited By: Pauline Megeke
Cover Concept & Illustration: Abel Murumba
Cover Design: Danielle Pitt
Layout Design: Kemunto Matunda

Note for Librarians:
A cataloguing record for this book is available from Library and Archives Canada.

ISBN: 978-1-926906-43-0

Dedication

To Inzu ya Masaaba, BaMasaaba of the Dispersion, House of Malele, Codvia Wakiro, Susan Kiguli, Mary Goretti Akol, Sebastian Jalameso, and George Watika.

Acknowledgements

I wish to express deep appreciation to the following for kindly reading through sections of the manuscript or all of it and making very useful suggestions: Ms Susan Khaitsa, Ms Carolyne Amuge, Mr. Moses Musingo, Dr. Danson Kahyana, and Dr. Patrick Mukakanya.

About the Author

Timothy Wangusa, PhD, studied English at Makerere University and the University of Leeds. Formerly Professor of Literature at Makerere, he has subsequently served as Research Professor at Uganda Christian University and Vice Chancellor of Kumi University in eastern Uganda. His writing career spans more than four decades, during which he has authored highly acclaimed works of both fiction and poetry. His poetic works include *A Pattern of Dust*, *Anthem for Africa* (translated into Italian, *Inno per l'Africa*) and *Africa's New Brood*. *Betwixt Mountain and Wilderness* is his second novel and comprises part of his project of the Mwambu Trilogy.

He has also completed works due for future publication, namely: *I Love You, You Beast!* (Reflections on Literature and Faith); and *Poems of Mount Elgon* (*Bilomelele bye Lukingi Masaaba*). Other works in progress include *A Poetic Map of Africa* (a literary study); and *Poetic Mix* (occasional and miscellaneous poems).

Professor Wangusa is currently Visiting Professor of Literature at Uganda Christian University and Vice Chair of LuMasaaba Language Academy. He is engaged in co-writing with Cornelius Wekunya the first *LuMasaaba Dictionary*, now at an advanced stage.

He posits that "Poetry is the mother tongue of mankind", while he perceives literature as a "verbal rendering of the human soul or community condition".

I
Naming the Baby

Once upon a sunset, abrupt news leapt from hilltop to hilltop as fast as a black dog is famed to run. And I Nalukano the story-teller was at the very spot and saw everything that happened. And I also met all the persons who thought and said and did all the thoughts and words and deeds that took place, and I moved with them everywhere in that strange land.

The abrupt news was what had just befallen Mwambu two hills away on his way home. The news reached his father just at the entrance to the homestead, as he was returning his cattle from the day's grazing; and it at the very same moment reached his mother as she was beginning to peel green bananas for supper. They both heard the same heart-piercing words from noisy talkers hurriedly walking past their house.

And now as he waited for his son's sudden homecoming, Masaaba was pacing up and down the homestead with a distraught face under the fading sun, a whirlwind of anger raging in his inside. For those broadcasters of nasty events had blurted out, to everybody they met on the way, how Mwambu was that very hour heading for his parents' home in a state of utter disgrace. And in consequence, the entire village of BuNabarwa was already abuzz with gossip about the novelty that had just assailed their ears.

'My fellow woman, have you heard what I have heard?' asked one woman.

'Yes, yes, I've heard!' replied the other.

Men were not left out in the talk of the day.

'My fellow man, have you heard what I've heard?'

1

'Yes, yes, I've heard! Or do you think you're the only one with ears that do what they were created to do?'

'No, of course I'm not. But who could have bolted like lightning and told you the news in less time than it takes dust to absorb saliva?'

'You ask as though you're ignorant of the speed at which words travel. Don't people say that the word outstripped Saawa in Bukweland and arrived before him in Masaabaland?'

'So they say, indeed! So they say.'

'And what do they say that the word did say on arrival?'

'The word said that Saawa had committed a terrible abomination in the homestead of the chief.'

'Yes, I also confirm that that's what the word said – that Saawa had crazily opened his posterior into the chief's food basket!'

'And so the stench of his foul deed was carried by the word on wings of the wind well ahead of him.'

'But what has just happened is, of course, something of a different posture.'

'Yes, yes, of course. It's something to do with the naked front of a man, not with his dirty behind or underside.'

*　　*　　*

Many are the fingers and toes on both hands and feet. And as many millet harvests had come and gone since the day the baby came crying into this world, crying and kicking and shaking his clenched tiny fists as though at some monstrous combatant that he could already see.

From time to time throughout his infant days, NaBusuulwa, his mother, remembered how the baby had cried for so much longer than any other baby in the village had ever cried upon leaving its mother's womb. *'Did the babies cry because they could already smell something bad, something terrible? Were they cries of protest or cries of grief?'* she wondered. Well, perhaps they cried because of one of these reasons, she told herself, or perhaps for none of them, perhaps for some other reason.

Ah, but how wonderful it was to be baby boy's mother! The baby boy had opened her womb, and made her the proud woman among women that she now was.

Returning to the homestead any day from digging in the field, or from fetching water from the spring, or harvesting a bunch of green plantain, or gathering firewood from the hillside, NaBusuulwa radiated with pure delight when the baby-sitter's song rippled into her ears.

Wolele	Lullaby
Wolele	Lullaby
Wolele, mulesi womwana	Lullaby, says baby's nurse
Mayi atsiile kamanana	Mummy has gone to get baby's food
Kan'akobole	She will come back
Kan'onuune	You will soon suck
Kan'onuune mulesi womwana	You will soon suck, says baby's nurse
Kona liilo	Fall asleep
Kona liilo	Fall asleep
Kona liilo, mulesi womwana	Fall asleep, says baby's nurse

The baby boy was lulled into sleep by the song in the daytime. But at night, throughout his first moon in the world, he cried and cried.

*　　　*　　　*

'What kind of baby is it?' asked the baby's father's aunt, who was visiting the homestead.

'It's a human baby,' the baby boy's father, Masaaba, naughtily answered.

'Of course it's a human baby,' the aunt jovially countered. 'But is it *isaaka* or *liwola*?'

Masaaba very well knew *isaaka* to be a sour vegetable with tiny leaves, and *liwola* to be a sweet vegetable with large leaves.

'But what's all this about babies being edible leaves?' he sallied, pretending ignorance.

'You know what I mean.'

'No, I don't know what you mean!'

'In that case, let me change my question. Is it a real baby or a frog?'

Masaaba was scandalised. 'What do you mean by "frog"?'

'I mean,' she continued, 'is it a child who will remain in our clan, and raise a roof over our heads, or one who will hop off like a frog – like I did – when I got married and got lost into another clan? Tell me, is the baby grandfather or grandmother?'

'It's grandfather,' Masaaba revealed, finally relenting.

'Ah, that's good!' breathed the aunt, visibly relieved. That's good!'

'But did I overhear NaBusuulwa say,' she continued, slightly changing the subject, 'that baby cries throughout the night? Does he have a name?'

'Yes, I've given him a name.

'What name?'

'That of my great grandfather's younger brother – Mweru.'

'Not Mweru!' the aunt exclaimed.

'Why not?' Masaaba could not hide his surprise.

'Because it's the wrong one for baby.'

'And why is that so?'

'The name belongs to our clan, and Mweru was indeed known to be the father of one son and five daughters. But it was also a widely whispered secret among the village women and men of his day that his younger brother fathered that son for him! So, the baby's crying is a definite sign that he has rejected the name and spirit of Mweru, who died without a son.'

On her instructions, Masaaba's aunt had the baby brought to her early in the evening. In a ritual exercise, she held him in her lap and spoke coaxingly to him.

By way of testing baby, she started speaking to him by invoking the name of the heir-less Mweru.

'Stop crying, Mweru, great grandfather of baby's father,' she intoned.

Despite the words, the baby continued crying. So she carried on with her coaxing incantations.

'Stop crying, Masika, elder brother of my great grandfather.'

The baby continued crying.

'Stop crying, Kundu...Kalamya...Kitutu...'

The baby continued crying.

'Stop crying, Mwambu, great grandfather of my great grandfather –'

The baby suddenly stopped crying.

'This is Mwambu our ancestor,' confidently pronounced Masaaba's aunt, returning baby to its mother. 'It's Mwambu our ancient ancestor who has come back in spirit and flesh. Welcome back Mwambu the Great One! she said.

*   *   *

It was that grey time of the evening between daylight and utter darkness when a traveller going past someone's homestead has to cough and announce, *'Ise niy'o'bira.'* 'It's me passing by.'

Emerging from the banana grove immediately below his father's house, Mwambu contrived a cough to signify his presence in the thickening night.

'Uhuh, uhuh –'

'Who's that?' Masaaba harshly inquired, at last halting his endless shuffling between the kitchen and the cattle pen.

'It's me,' Mwambu expressionlessly replied. He removed his bag from his shoulder and set it on the veranda.

'NaBusuulwa!' Masaaba gruffly called to his wife, unsure in that instant whether at once to use his hands on Mwambu. 'You come out of the house - your son is here.'

'*My* son, did you say?' NaBusuulwa protested. 'Has he suddenly stopped being your son and become mine because of what has happened?' She came out to find father and son silently standing at the threshold to the house, each apparently still looking for the first words to say.

'Sit down, Mwambu,' she instinctively directed him, something in her prompting her to play the role of the mediator despite her own unspeakable disappointment at what Mwambu had done. 'You too should sit down,' she told Masaaba, pointing the two to the wooden *musesa* folding chairs on the veranda. She then sat herself with a sigh on the grass directly opposite the doorway.

'Mwambu, is it true, what we have heard?' Masaaba asked, more in distress than anger.

Mwambu looked down and gave no answer.

'Is it true that you were stripped naked at Mandu's home on your way here by gangsters who wanted you circumcised?'

Again Mwambu gave no answer. Looking away from his father to his mother, he took the chair nearer her and sat down.

'And is it true, Mwambu, that you were circumcised at school?'

'No,' Mwambu cleverly replied, 'I was not circumcised at school.'

'So it is a false rumour?' Masaaba incredulously asked. 'The villagers have just made it up for fun?'

'No, it is not a rumour,' Mwambu said. 'I have been circumcised, but it was not at school.'

'*Where* were you circumcised?' Masaaba flared. He now let go his restrained temper.

'In Elgonton town.'

'Not even on the school compound but in Elgonton town?' he aspirated.

'Yes, father.'

'Don't father-father me!' Masaaba reeled with exasperation. 'I'm no father of yours, and you're no son of mine!'

Then whose son am I? Mwambu thought in a flash of intuition.

'That is not a good thing to say,' NaBusuulwa anxiously interjected, as some unspoken thing trembled at the very core of her being. 'Your words could become a curse.'

'Shut up, you!' Masaaba shouted, diverting his fury to his wife. 'This is no son of mine, I say! Will you go in and light the lamp instead of crossing me in what I say?'

NaBusuulwa entered the house to look for the hurricane lamp.

'Tell me,' Masaaba continued, turning to Mwambu, 'On the compound of which father of yours did you stand in Elgonton?'

No answer.

'On the grave of which of your ancestors was libation poured?'

No answer.

'What's the name of your circumciser?'

No answer.

'And who purified your hands with unfermented beer? Who prayed for you and your children and your children's children to be fruitful, healthy and prosperous? Answer me, Mwambu, who did all these things for you?'

But Mwambu gave no answer, and no answer was needed. For Masaaba knew too well by now that his son had had a white man's circumcision, lying on his back inside a concrete building, his eyes fixed – not on the mountain of ancients on the horizon where the sun comes from, but on the underside of a roof.

'Follow your mother into the house, Mwambu,' Masaaba directed with a dismissive wave of the hand, walking away towards the cattle pen.

'But before you do that,' Masaaba remembered to ask, 'how is it that you have come home today? Didn't you tell us it is tomorrow that you would finally return, after finishing to read all the books in the school?'

'Yes, I told you that,' replied Mwambu.

'So is this tomorrow, according to you?'

'No, today is not tomorrow.'

'Then why did you not wait to come tomorrow? Was a baby whom you were hurrying to return and breastfeed crying here at home?'

Mwambu winced at the thought of his having to breastfeed like a woman, and was repelled by his father's insinuation.

'No,' he uneasily replied. 'It's just that I had finished writing the Cambridge School Certificate examinations, and I, together with my classmates, was doing nothing useful after that. I, therefore, decided to come home today.'

He dared not tell his father that he had also written a nasty letter about his former girlfriend Nambozo and the school chaplain copulating in the chapel vestry. He had posted the letter on the school notice-board, while the rest of the school was having lunch, before taking off for fear of harsh reprisal if he was apprehended still lingering within the school compound.

While Mwambu entered the house to join his mother, Masaaba walked away into the dark to go and secure the entrance to his cattle pen of a handful of cows and their bull. And he was bitterly thinking: *Why did it have to be Masaaba's son? Why had Mwambu to be the first boy in the clan to be circumcised without the father's knowledge? Why? Why? What a curse to descend upon my roof! What a misfortune to ...*

He hit the big toe of his left foot against a log he had earlier meant to lean against the nearby ash tree. He bravely sucked in the pain through gritted teeth at the same instant as he thought of Munyelezi, the first man in the clan to be circumcised indoors while lying on his back in a hospital like a white man. As a result, Munyelezi was derisively re-named "Musungu" (white man) by the villagers. To all the people of the mountain country, that circumcision season of 1938, that saw the first hospital circumcisions, was known ever thereafter as Operating Table.

'And that was the very year,' Masaaba ruefully reminded himself as he walked back from the cattle pen to the house, 'in which Mwambu started going to school.'

II
Naming the Season

On the agenda of the first meeting of Elgonton District Committee for the year 1951 there were two main items: naming the last circumcision season; and bursaries for schools and colleges. As committee members arrived one by one, they hang about the committee hall noisily exchanging personal news as well as pleasant nothings from their various localities.

'Gentlemen Members,' the Chairman called out at the opportune moment, 'let me now call the meeting to order, at exactly 9.30 a.m.'

By right of office, the Secretary General of the district was automatically also the District Committee Chairman. Having commenced his administrative career as sub-county chief years back, Joel Masolo was now holding the highest native office in the district, immediately below that of the colonial District Commissioner.

'Under Communication from the Chair, let me begin,' he said, 'by first welcoming the three Members newly appointed to the District Committee by His Majesty the King's representative in the district. All three are, by interesting coincidence, survivors of the Second World War, who bravely fought for the British Empire and won the war. I shall ask them to stand up one by one to greet the Members of the Committee.

The previously serving Members turned their heads around the hall to see who the new appointees were.

'They are,' the Chairman read out: 'Peter Wayelo from Namisindwa..., John Wambooza from BuTandiga..., and Patrick Kuloba from BuSukuya.'

11

As each Member stood up, the entire council gave him a due handclap.

'Next, still under Communication from the Chair, it is with much surprised pleasure,' announced the Chairman, 'that I have to inform this Committee that a child of this soil, Abraham Mwambu son of Masaaba in BuSukuya County, has become the first school-goer from Elgonton District to be admitted to the highest point of finding out, to that Dream-house of Knowing called Makerere, to read and read and read books till he obtains a very big prize called a degree.'

There was spontaneous clapping of hands, loud and long, mixed with jumbled words of admiration and wonder.

'Let's express our excitement and pleasure in our usual manner,' resumed the Chairman after the noise had died down, 'and be very smart about it. One –'

There followed a rhythmic pah pah pah of hands...

'Two –'

Another bout of thunderous pah pah pah...

'Three –'

A final, prolonged bout...

'Thank you, thank you, thank you,' the Chairman shouted. 'Thank you, gentlemen Members!

'And now,' he continued, 'if I may pronounce a few words in this connection. You Members will definitely be pleased to confirm to yourselves that Mwambu's pioneering of the path to that faraway legend known as Makerere, which most of us just hear about, has killed the foolish talk by some people that students from Elgonton District have had their brains ruined by circumcision! They have been claiming that as long as circumcision continues its ancient grip upon the slopes of this mountain, none of our sons and daughters will ever reach Makerere's war front to fight in the final battle with books. It was nonsensical talk. Circumcision is not an enemy of books and pens. But neither is it a mysterious cure for those of us having cow-dung instead of brains inside their skulls.'

The Members burst into happy laughter, each imagining how the majority of his fellow Committee Members, possibly all of them with the exception of himself, might be carrying such contents inside their own skulls.

'But excuse me, Mr. Chairman,' called Member John Wambooza, raising his hand. 'May I ask a question?'

'Yes, the new Member from BuTandiga,' granted the Chairman. 'You may ask your maiden question.'

The eyes of all the Members were turned on this newcomer Member who seemed to be so self-advancing as to want to be the first person to be heard on the floor of the Committee hall for that Committee session.

'It's O.K. for you to announce that Mwambu is going to that Makerere that sounds like it is your God, but what was his conduct like as a student at Elgonton Secondary School? Do we know?'

'That's none of this Committee's business,' flatly pronounced the Chairman. 'Sit down, Member Wambooza.'

'Not yet, Mr. Chairman,' protested Wambooza, remaining on his feet. 'I happen to know that the conduct of this Mwambu of yours in his last term at Elgonton Secondary School was that of a very rotten animal. He should have been expelled from the school, but he had already sat for his examinations by the time he committed his worst act of misconduct. Is this the rascal on whom this Committee is going to spend a fat bursary?'

'And what's the source of your information, Member Wambooza?' inquired the somewhat irritated Chairman.

'My younger sister, whose name is Nambozo,' declared Wambooza, unwittingly dropping a sexual innuendo and instantly sending the Committee into spontaneous, prolonged laughter.

'I can already see, Mr. Chairman,' Wambooza sneered, 'that Members of this Committee laugh at anything! But it's not an amusing matter that I'm bringing up, Mr. Chairman. Let me tell you that the two of them – that's to say, my sister Nambozo and that Mwambu – were in the same class, Mr. Chairman. That's how he came to endanger my sister, Mr. Chairman. Nambozo herself could tell this Committee the ugly truth if she was brought here and you questioned her. Her future chances for reading more books were almost ruined completely through the malice of that Mwambu.'

'How, how?' interjected a hoarse voice from somewhere in the middle of the hall.

'Order, order, Members!' the Chairman called out.

'So that Mwambu of yours is not such wonderful news Mr. Chairman,' Wambooza concluded before sitting down. 'In fact, he's really bad news.'

'*Wututu ari bikhale'byo!*' shouted a voice from the back row, meaning that Wututu the commonsensical bird would dismissively say 'What bygone stuff!' to Wambooza's story.

'In any case,' the Chairman observed, concurring with the voice from the back row, 'this Committee has no official communication from Elgonton Secondary School on the matter, and Mwambu is no longer under the rules of that school.'

'My question is different, Mr Chairman,' announced Wayelo, jumping to his feet without waiting for the go-ahead. 'They say that a twisted tree became twisted at germination –'

'*N'inula yaama nyana!* And the animal that is sweet,' the Chairman contrarily cut in, 'was already sweet in its infancy.'

'That may well be so, Mr. Chairman. But it appears that this Mwambu has never changed from the little devil that he was in Primary One. Because you see, Mr. Chairman, I was with him at Namwombe Primary School in the same class and – yes, yes, and the Members shouldn't murmur. He was a mean-looking boy,' he exaggerated on account of his permanent dislike for Mwambu, 'who always put up his hand to answer every question and any question, and so he got the whole class to gang against him and bully him for knowing everything.'

To the amused Members, the rough-grained and slightly balding Wayelo certainly looked as old as a man who had eaten twice as many millet granaries as those eaten by a boy who has just completed secondary school.

'But we all know the saying which states that to ask is not bad, Mr. Chairman,' Wayelo carried on, his elbows proudly sticking outwards. 'Therefore, I'm not ashamed to ask as I'm going to ask.'

'Yes, ask your question,' the Chairman egged him on.

'What is it that Mwambu is going to get from Makerere? I want to know if it's something good or just rubbish. Is it a decoration, a *kyepe,* a medal such as some of us got from the King's African Rifles – KAR, popularly known as KEYA – for distinguished service on the field of battle in the Second World War? Tell me, Mr. Chairman, what's this thing they call *Diguli*?

Some Members hissed and mumbled their surprise at the new Member's apparent brave ignorance.

'That's a very good question,' sarcastically remarked the Chairman. 'Sit down, Member. Is there anyone who can tell the Member what, in the Pinkman's language, is called a Degree? Yes, the Member for BuNetaya.'

'As many fellow Members know,' BuNetaya's Member announced with an air of self-congratulation, 'my own nephew, the son of my sister who is married in the plains of BuGwere, is in his second year at Makerere. I have been there to visit him, and I tell you Members – you should see the books that those children read! Books with very big letters, books with very small letters, very fat books, and very old books – they read them all. There's a very, very huge building, ten times the size of this Committee Hall, which is full of nothing but books. Those children read and read and read until all those books are in their heads! And when they have read all those books, Mr. Chairman, that *is* what a degree is.'

'Nonsense!' shouted the Member for BuNezekeze, shooting up. 'That's not a degree! I wonder how some people talk. Fat books and old books in the children's heads indeed! Who doesn't know that a degree is a big piece of cloth? It's an overflowing black sheet of cloth, which those who have been to Makerere of Uganda, or to Makerere of England which is known as Cambridge, wear on top of their shirts and trousers. It's like the big black cloth that priests wear on Sunday.'

'Mr. Chairman,' interposed the Member for BuNasuufwa, 'if that's a degree, then all priests have degrees! Is that what the Member is claiming?'

'I don't think so,' replied the Chairman.

'Mr. Chairman,' the Member for BuNasuufwa continued, 'let me inform the whole Committee of the right thing. A degree is a hat.'

'What!' chorused the majority of the Members.

'Yes,' re-affirmed the Member for BuNasuufwa, 'a degree is a hat. Let me tell you. Most of you know the Reverend Graves of Elgonton Secondary School. On Sunday he wears a black gown, which my brother from BuNezekeze would call a degree, but that's not a degree. On Parents' Day, however, he wears a funny black hat with four corners and tassels like those of a maize cob.

That's when he is wearing a degree.'

'If that's so, Mr. Chairman,' the Member for BuNezekeze rallied, 'then we would be right to claim that the dirty banana fibre hat with corners, which Nataka the illiterate beggar of BuWabwala wears on his head, is a degree!'

An uproar of laughter ensued. For Nataka was well known all over Elgonton District as the ragged beggar with elephantine legs who was forever on his feet collecting rumours and gossip from important people in one locality and broadcasting them in another locality as prophecy – in exchange for a coin or a piece of cassava.

'Well, Mr. Chairman,' declared Wayelo, jumping up one more time, 'if *Diguli* is no better than Nataka's hat, then that Mwambu can go ahead and get one at once!'

*   *   *

Coming to the last substantive item on the agenda, the Chairman first briefed the Members on the procedure for proposing names for the previous circumcision season.

'When you stand up to propose a term or name,' he announced, 'begin by giving your name and telling us where you come from – for record purposes. Then you tell the Committee the name of your own circumcision year. Next, you propose the term you wish to recommend. If necessary, you briefly explain the term or the phenomenon you wish to be commemorated. And then, without talking round and round, you sit down!

'Needless to remind you,' he continued, 'the term or name you propose must have something to do with some major occurrence in the district, the country, or the world since the previous circumcision season. It may be some hardship, innovation, wonder or bounty that the people of this mountain land have seen, learnt, encountered, undertaken, suffered or enjoyed in the recent past.'

Several hands shot up as soon as the Chairman finished speaking.

'Yes, Member number one.'

'I am Wefwafwa from BuNezekeze. I was eaten by the knife in the year of Rats' Tails. That is the year when tails of rats were required to be produced by every man with a home towards the government's fight against the plague caused by rats. If you produced a rat's tail, it was assumed that you had killed the rat that owned that tail, and you did not have to turn up with the entire carcass of that rat at the local administration headquarters to prove what you had accomplished.

'My proposal for the last circumcision season,' the Member continued, 'is "Landslides". My reason for the choice is that, as all Members know, last year our mountain slopes were scarred by landslides to an extent we have never seen before. But there was also a funny side to the landslides, Mr. Chairman. In BuNezekeze, one morning a certain family found that its entire house and banana plantation had slid down the hillside and had been superimposed intact over somebody else's land in the valley below. To the astonished new neighbour, the head of the equally astonished new arrivals said, "Please stop shouting that I've invaded part of your land. As you can see, I've come with my own house, land and crops!"'

The entire Committee burst into uproarious laughter.

'Member number two,' the Chairman routinely called, pointing to one of the raised hands.

'My name is Wameela from BuMasiifwa. I paid my debt to the Mountain in the year of the Aeroplane. That is when the first aeroplane to ever fly across our land was sighted. And, Mr. Chairman, what an astounding marvel that was! A thundering, roaring gigantic metallic bird catapulting away up in the sky, at an altitude higher than any eagle had ever risen, and excreting from its rear a fantastic trail of thick white smoke that lingered behind long after the plane had disappeared from our view.

'My choice of a name for the last circumcision festival,' announced the Member, is "Sunset at Sunrise". The pink men call it "Eclipse". We all remember the day last year when the sun disappeared soon after it had risen! In the darkness that engulfed the land, children setting out for school and women beginning to hoe the fields, all started running back home. Chicken returned to the houses to roost. And you remember how some scaremongers quickly went around claiming that the sun was going to stay away for many, many moons!'

'Member number three...

'Member number four...

'Member number five...

'Member number six...

'Member number seven...

'Member number eight...

'Member number nine...

'Member number ten...

'Member number eleven...

'Member number twelve...

'Member number thirteen...

'Member number fourteen.

'Member number fifteen, and who will be the last to speak on the subject on the floor.'

Thereafter, the Chairman allowed some brief discussions on the fifteen proposed names.

'Mr. Chairman,' observed one elderly Member, 'from all the important occurrences in the last two years so far put forward, it seems to me that the deepest one is that of our son who has become the first from this mountain to go on a warrior's adventure in pursuit of the Spirit of Knowingness in the faraway land of the plains, following the trail of Kundu, his ancestor who always wanted to find out some more.'

'I concur on that point, Mr. Chairman!' was the enthusiastic support from another elderly Member. The Chairman signalled him to get up and elaborate on his contribution.

'I propose,' he said, 'that the name that we need should be chosen from one of these three: One – Cambridge, which is the name of the first monster that Mwambu has killed; Two – Makerere, which is the name of the second monster that Mwambu is going to engage in battle; and Three – Degree, which is the name of the third monster that Mwambu is going to conquer at the end of his war against the Giants of Unknowingness.'

After brief exchanges among the Members, consensus seemed to favour Cambridge, popularly indigenised as "Kamburikyi".

'Is it the wish of all the Members,' asked the Chairman, 'that we settle for the name "Kwa Kamburikyi"?'

'No!' Wambooza angrily shouted without getting up. 'It's not the wish of *all* the Members!'

'Hands up,' the Chairman coolly directed, 'those who are for "Kwa Kamburikyi".

All hands except three went up.

'Hands up those who are against.'

Two hands went up. They were those of Wambooza and Wayelo.

'Hands up any abstentions.'

The lone hand of Patrick Kuloba went up. All the Members turned their eyes onto him, some wondering how the Member who hailed from the same county and sub-county as Mwambu could be the very one to abstain from voting, one way or the other, on the name that was in honour to the pioneering young scholar who was the pride of the entire mountain.

Known only to Wayelo, were two small facts: that Mwambu's father and Kuloba's father were brothers, Kuloba's being the elder; and that Mwambu had also had his secret hospital circumcision during the very season that was being named.

And deep in his inside, Kuloba was smarting and thinking: *It is true what they say – as your brother procreates, you must also procreate. This Mwambu who is young enough to be my son, or is perhaps my son, I am yet to properly punish him for having jumped into my bed with Mayuba, my wife, while I was away fighting the war of the red men...I'm sure the right moment will come someday...*

'With those three exceptions,' the Chairman ruled, giving Kuloba a sardonic smile for being the most awkward voter of the day, 'it's hereby resolved by a clear majority of Elgonton District Committee that the previous circumcision year be named and be known forever and ever as "Kwa Kamburikyi".'

III
The Sealed Envelope

The admission letter to the Hill of Knowledge, as its students fondly called it, was posted to Mwambu at the address of his former school, Elgonton Secondary School, via the District Committee. A written note from the District Committee office conveyed the Committee's warm congratulations to him upon his 'pioneering performance', for which he was being offered a District Scholarship. It further urged him to collect the admission letter from the school immediately.

And so it was that three days later, Mwambu found himself retracing his steps to the school he had left in a frenzy months back, swearing never to go back there in the foreseeable future for anything under the sun.

'I understand that there is a letter here for me,' he said in a rehearsed matter-of-fact tone to the young woman he presumed to be the head teacher's new secretary, after the formal greeting. 'May I please have it?'

'Yes, you certainly may. What's your name?

'Mwambu.'

'Aha, you are Abraham Mwambu!' exclaimed the young woman, who had never seen Mwambu before, and had just come straight from a secretarial college in the north of England to take up her first job ever.

Mwambu was thrown into confusion. 'You're surprised that that's my name?' he asked as coolly as he could.

She blushed slightly.

'No, um, yes, no!' she haltingly replied. 'It's just that I have a note here in red ink from Mr. Bentley instructing me to refer you to him when you come to collect your admission letter.'

'A note in red, did you say?'

'Yes, I'm afraid that is so.'

Mwambu instantly recalled the school punishment that was called 'Reds'. The worst form of punishment for offending students was, of course, manual labour, followed by strokes of the cane. 'Reds' took third position, and consisted of a student having to write on paper as many lines of words in red ink as satisfied the teacher administering the punishment. So a punishment in 'Reds' might be announced as '100 Reds' or '1,000 Reds'.

'But I should tell you,' the secretary went on, 'that Mr. Bentley is not yet in office. You may have to walk around your old school and come back after about one hour.'

*　　*　　*

A note in red...100 Reds...1,000 Reds...1,000,000 Reds...red blood...red cloth...red as a burning fire...red skin of 'white' people...red eyes...like those of a cock... red sun when seen through smoke... a note in red...a note in red...red flowers of flame trees ...a note in red...red as hell...a note in red...a note in red –

He had just walked past the classrooms when the library springing into view interrupted his thoughts. And off skipped his mind to his second year in the school, to the morning he encountered the most unforgettable book.

He could see himself reading in the library that fantastic morning. He has been developing into an avid consumer of fiction and science readers. This morning he has by sheer chance just taken down from some shelf the book entitled *The Radium Woman*. He wonders, what's a radium woman? He knows radio, radius, radiant...is she radiant? If so, then she must be very beautiful, very lovely. But it says on the inside of the front flap: 'This is the story of Madam Curie...' And this is another puzzle. Is the story about a curious woman? For sure he knows the word 'curious'. And why is she Madam, and not Lady Curie? His eyes go back to the beginning of the first line. 'This is the story of Madam Curie, a Polish woman scientist who discovered radium, and was twice a Nobel Prize winner – for Chemistry, and for Physics.' And now he is as curious as Madam Curie. What is radium? What is Nobel? What makes a prize to be called Nobel? He reads on and is told radium is a radioactive element. He tries to figure out the element: is it to do with radios? Is it the element that makes radios active, that makes them work?

He decides to flip through the book. Not browsing but mostly looking at chapter headings in the first place. And then the words hit him with a brain hammer –

I Take the Sun and Throw It!

'What!' He violently pulls himself up and jerks his head. 'What! *Take* the sun and *throw* it?' He stands up and walks to the window, oblivious of other students reading around him, and looks at the late morning sun in the blue sky. '*Take* the sun and *throw* it...? Take it...Who...In what hand...With what force.... Throw it *where...*? *Take* the sun and *throw* it...?

All the incredible achievements of impossible things as narrated in fireside stories from his childhood rose tumultuously in his mind – Monster's magic belt leaping across the wilderness to go catch a run-away trickster...a tiny human being slaying the gigantic Monster...a dead human being springing back to life the very instant that *lufufu,* the resurrection herb, is applied to his corpse or any tiny bit of his remains!

I Take the Sun and Throw It! With seething brain he sits down at the table and reads the book right through, skipping lunch and afternoon classes and evening tea break till he finishes it. Madam Curie! Radium Woman! Wife, mother, scientist of lofty imaginings, lofty ambition, lofty perseverance! Pathfinder and discoverer, who plies through heaps, tonnes of mud for years on end, looking for this illusive, unknown thing. Till at last she arrives at it. She isolates particles of it. Eureka! *Radium* has been found! A new, radiant and body-piercing element has been discovered!

Woman of knowledge, truth and freedom! Toiling in her laboratory through years of Poland's imperial enslavement, and living long enough to witness the day of Poland's hard-won political liberty; such that she can say with infinite relief, 'And so we, who were born in servitude and chained to our cradles, have at last seen the salvation of our country!'

Yes – Mwambu concludes, hypnotised and convinced – *she could take the sun and throw it*! Yes, she could. She could rest it on the far end of a long, long lever, pivot it upon some appropriate planet, and then – fling it outside space...!

'...And *where* is that?' he wondered. 'Where is *outside* space...? What does it mean to be *outside space*...? And what would become of *our world without the sun*...?' He wondered. He wondered and shuddered.

*　　*　　*

Then one day at the end of the third year of high school, the Physics teacher announced that the subject of the lesson he was commencing on was Light. He then immediately surprised the whole class by putting the question –

'Has any of you ever seen the sun?'

What a childish question, each one thought.

But everybody knew that Mr. Ian Browne was a very tricky teacher. No one could predict his remarks, actions and moods with any degree of accuracy. He was a very clever man with machines, and especially gifted as a repairer of clocks and electronic instruments, besides being extremely deft at playing the chapel organ, which his missionary father living in neighbouring Kenya Colony had piously donated to the school. But he was a man of opposites: hot-tempered and kind, abusive and publicly repentant. The students accordingly gave him the love-hate nickname of 'Saint Brute', sometimes just reduced to 'Brute'.

Seeing that he was getting no response, Mr. Browne changed the wording of his question.

'Has any of you ever looked at the sun?'

Amused silence was all he got. They were not going to let him catch them up so easily.

'Hands up!' he bellowed. 'Has any of you *ever looked at the sun*?'

Three unwilling hands went up.

'Yes, Moit.'

'Sir, did you say,' Moit asked, '"seen" or "looked at"?'

'Don't answer a question with a question! Let me have another attempt at an answer.'

Mwambu's hand went up.

'Yes, Mwambu.'

'Yes, sir, I have countless times looked at the sun.'

'Then you're very foolish,' came Mr. Browne's quick rejoinder. 'You should never look at the sun with your naked eyes!'

The class gave out some hollow laugh, but it was more at Mr. Browne than at Mwambu.

'Because if you stare at the sun with your naked eyes,' Mr. Browne waxed on, 'you will ruin your eyesight.'

What a brute insult! Mwambu told himself. In his vexation he stood up without asking for permission.

'But, sir, that's very unfair of you!'

The entire class turned to gape at Mwambu. No one had ever dared to say such a thing to Mr. Browne's face.

'Because, sir, you did not ask me if I have ever looked at the sun with my naked eyes. And as my eyesight has never been ruined –'

'Don't answer back!' Mr. Browne yelled. 'Never you answer me back, do you hear? And sit down at once – you're wasting everybody's time!'

And down did Mwambu sit, seething with rage. His mind revolted. And he switched off his ears from Mr. Browne's lesson. *What a cheap question! This blind guide of those with very good eyes...comes all the way across the seas... to ask us if we have ever seen the sun! What an idiotic question! How many people has he seen around here... who have lost their eyesight... because of looking at the sun...looking up to the sun...living under the sun... rejoicing under the sun...talking to the sun...clapping to the sun...singing to the sun...dancing to the sun...praying to the sun...*

Mr. Browne was by now talking about *opaqueness* and *transparency* and *translucency* and *reflection* and *refraction* and *cuboids, spheres, hemispheres, pyramids* and *triangular* and *poly-angular prisms* and *retardation* of light as it *transmits through heavier medium* and...

But Mwambu only caught fragments of all this, as he was still nursing his anger. Then all of a sudden he felt the urge to ask Mr. Browne just one question, since he was apparently going on and on about light and sources of light. Suddenly, he shot up his hand right in the middle of Mr. Browne's ongoing sentence –

'Yes, you Mwambu there. Do you have a question?'

'Yes, sir,' he exhaled, his facial muscles twitching with the hate of injured pride. *'Can you take the sun and throw it?'*

'What!' shouted Mr. Browne going utterly red as the rest of the class giggled and turned to look at the formulator of the weird question.

'Sir, if I may repeat the question: *Can you take the sun and throw it?'*

'Mwambu, you are mad!' Mr. Browne shouted again. 'What kind of stupid question is that? Sit down!'

'But sir,' Mwambu cheekily dared, 'you have not answered my question.'

'Get out of my class!' barked Mr. Browne, infuriated and charging towards him. 'Quick, out of my class!'

In a flash, Mwambu jumped onto his space of the shared bench where he had been sitting, onto the top of the desk, into the isle next to the one down which Mr. Browne was charging, ducked to avoid the blackboard duster Mr. Browne flung at him, and out he dashed through the half open, grinning door.

Within an hour, the pupils knew, Saint Brute's temper would be gone, and Mwambu would be back in the next class after a good dressing down disguised as 'spiritual counselling'.

* * *

Upon returning to the headmaster's office, Mwambu was informed by the secretary that Mr. Bentley was indeed now in and could be seen. A little nervous at having to see the head teacher well known for his austere personality, he knocked on the door of the inner room.

'Come in!' shouted Mr. Bentley in a strong and clear voice.

And there behind a table crowded with files and loose paper sat the figure of Mr. Arthur Bentley the Head teacher, his eyes professorially peeping over his gold-rimmed spectacles. Above him at the back on the wall hang a portrait of King George VI, *by the grace of God* the proud King of Great Britain and Northern Ireland, the Dominions of Canada, Australia and New Zealand, the Colonies, Protectorates, Trustee-ships, and Properties of the British Empire so vast that the sun never set upon it!

Below the portrait of His Majesty the King was a plaque of the British national anthem in golden letters, the words of which Mwambu was very familiar with. Just now his eyes fell on the middle stanza, with its seemingly pagan message of hatred of 'those who are not for us':

> O Lord our God, arise,
> Scatter our enemies,
>   And make them fall;
> Confound their politics,
> Frustrate their knavish tricks;
> On Thee our hopes we fix:
>   God save the King!

'Good morning, young man,' Mr. Bentley routinely greeted Mwambu in the well-practised official voice of close to thirty years at Elgonton.

'Good morning, sir.'

Mr. Bentley tactically feigned ignorance of which past student was standing before him; yet he had a reputation for knowing all the top class students by name and face from year to year.

'What's your name?' he asked with a slight narrowing of the eyes.

'Mwambu.'

'That's right. And what's your first name?'

'Kiboole,' replied Mwambu with a straight face.

'What!' Mr. Bentley exclaimed. 'After six years in Junior

Secondary and Senior Secondary school at Elgonton, you still don't know what a first name is?'

'Yes, sir, I think I know,' Mwambu bravely replied.

'Then, if you are the Mwambu who was in top class here last year,' Mr. Bentley informed him, 'your first name is Abraham.'

'Thank you, sir,' Mwambu contrived to say. 'But, sir, that's my fourth name. My first name, given me before I was born, is Kiboole, which means First-born.'

'Are you giving me a lecture, you boy,' Mr. Bentley archly asked, 'on local folklore and black arts?'

'No, sir! And my second name is Mwambu, from my clan, given to me at birth. My third one, sir, is Masaaba, after my father. Then when I was ten years old, sir, I was given my fourth name of Abraham, which I've even recently re-...'

'Do you know, young man,' Mr. Bentley angrily cut in, 'that you're here to collect your testimonial for Makerere?'

Mwambu was still standing on the same spot where he had stopped after entering Mr. Bentley's office. In Mr. Bentley's judgement, he did not qualify for the guests' chair, just one foot away.

'Yes, sir, that's for what I'm here.'

'Listen to your English!' fumed Mr. Bentley. 'What kind of sentence construction is that? You should say, "That's what I'm here for." '

'Sir, it's because here at Elgonton,' Mwambu countered with acted innocence, 'we were taught, as a rule, never to end an English sentence with a preposition, such as "for". The teacher even quoted the big man Winston Churchill, being ignorant of the rule at first, as venting his dislike of it by saying, "That's a rule *up with which* I'll not put!" Truly, sir, that's what we were taught by the Reverend Graves when...'

'Shut up!' shouted Mr. Bentley, straightening himself up in his chair as if about to get onto his feet. Mwambu involuntarily moved back one pace towards the closed door, sensing some brewing storm.

'The Reverend Graves is a teacher of Mathematics and the Bible, not English. And get his name out of your filthy head once and for all! Do you *h-e-a-r*?'

'Ye-yes, sir! Ye-yes, sir!' stammered Mwambu.

'And you very well know what devilish lie you dreamt up about him, called it a revelation, wrote it out, and posted it up on the school notice-board! What diseased brain do you carry inside that skull? A sick daydreamer who claims to be a seer of visions! Do you know the difference between dreams and revelations, you young rascal?

'Yes, sir, I think I know the difference. It's in the Bible.'

'You dare invoke the Bible, you incorrigible, unrepentant sinner?' Mr. Bentley was by now beside himself with rage. Superiorly pouting his mouth, he sarcastically asked, 'In what book and verse did you learn this, you gangster?'

'The Book of Prophet Joel,' Mwambu coolly answered, 'Chapter 2, verse 28.'

'And what does it say, Mr. *Theologian*?' Mr. Bentley sneered.

'I quote, sir. "In the latter day, I will pour out my spirit upon all flesh. Your sons and daughters shall prophesy, your old men shall dream dreams, and your young men shall see visions." '

'And what does that *mean* to you, *Professor* Mwambu?' The irritation in his sarcastic voice was approaching breaking point.

'Sir, that whereas what we young men see in visions are true revelations,' Mwambu enunciated with boyish tongue-in-cheek and with what appeared to Mr. Bentley like the slightest nod of the head towards himself and therefore encompassing him, 'what old men dream are mere dreams of...'

'Out! Out! Out of my office!'

Mr. Bentley rose to his feet in a fury, charged towards the door, while Mwambu chaotically stepped aside to let him pass, flung the door open, and rigidly pointed him out with his left hand, while his right one held the door knob.

'Out you go!' he commanded at the top of his voice. 'Miss Gould,' he said to his dumbfounded secretary, 'give him that sealed envelope addressed to the Registrar of Makerere University College, with the initials "A.M." in the top left corner.

'Off you go, you scam!' He pushed him out of the outer door.

'And permanent curses upon you,' he raved on, 'if you dare to open that envelope and read its contents! It's not addressed to you, you rogue, you miscreant, you nincompoop, you scoundrel, you son of a b----, do you *h-e-a-r*?

IV
Journeying with the Sun

The Elgonton-Kampala bus settled to a steady rhythm on its westward journey to the city that Mwambu would be seeing for the first time. Lulled by that rhythm, he closed his eyes and went into a reverie. A filmstrip of his infant and school years passed before his inner eyes. The village where he first opened his eyes on the world, Namwombe Primary School, Elgonton Secondary School, fondly shortened to Egosec. At Egosec, the filmstrip is held to a pause: and he is with his friends of the Mountaineering Club and Elgonton Historical Club. He goes mountaineering with his Form Three classmates, and at night before they fall asleep under a tree he offers to say a prayer he has been composing, full of repeated sounds –

Stay with us, Lord, for the day is far spent; and yet the night is no night with you, but shines and shines on toward the perfect day. Defend us as you did defend Daniel in the dismal dungeon of deadly dragons; and seal our souls, O Saviour, with sweet, sound and silent sleep...

The filmstrip moves a little, and then pauses again. He is in a circle of the Historical Club members, with their teacher and patron at the centre of the circle. He is Mr. Suuya, endearingly nick-named 'Mr. Written Word', who once bluntly pronounced that *a people without recorded history are a guesswork people.*

'And so, Mr. Suuya, when and how did Masaaba's Mountain become Mount Elgon?'

'Let me answer you like this. Masaaba the owner of this mountain had one daughter, in addition to his three sons. Her name was Nagudi. She was married back into the tribe of her mother Nabarwa, the Kalenjin. Nagudi's husband was Gony. He was a heroic warrior and a man of great substance. Trekking from the sea and arriving on the sunrise side of Masaaba's Mountain, the first pink man asked the hundredth generation of Nagudi's offspring as to what they called their mountain. 'Gony's Mountain - El Gony,' they said. The pink man wrote down on a piece of paper what he thought he had heard – 'Elgon' – and sent the piece of paper back to the map-makers in his country. That's how Masaaba's Mountain became 'Mount Elgon'.

And then there were those weekend visits by Wakhale (nick-named 'Antiquity'), Nambozo and himself to old men and women with long memory to try and crosscheck the origins of their people, in the hope of writing it all down one day.

'Tell us, old one, when did we the inhabitants of this mountain start to exist?'

'We never started. We have always been there.'

'But where did we live before we came to this mountain?'

'We never lived anywhere else. We have always lived here. Masaaba's father, Mundu, rose from the ground through a hole somewhere near the top of the mountain.'

'Where is that hole? Could you go and show it to us?'

'No! They say that the hole is nowadays a deep lake of fresh water.'

'But when did that hole appear in the ground, and when did Mundu come out of it?'

'Go and ask that one to the Creator, not me! No one was there except the Creator himself and Mundu.

'All right, all right, old one. We did not mean to ask you only what we should ask the Creator. But was the Creator there a long time or a short time before Mundu came out of the hole?'

'And now you want me to utter foolishness! Next you will ask me if the Creator also came out of that same hole! Or out of a hole in the sky, and if I saw him arriving! He is the moulder; we are the outcome of his moulding. He is the begetter; we are his issue. Do you want me to disgrace myself before him?'

'No, no, we want you to do no such thing. But tell us about the people of the plains – the Iteso and BaGwere. Were they not there when Mundu came out of the hole?'

'What! The Iteso and BaGwere – of all the peoples! I have told you that no one else was there. The peoples of the plains came only yesterday. They came swarming towards the mountain from the wilderness beyond. They wanted to settle on the mountain but we repulsed them in the fiercest battle that has ever been fought on earth!'

'Who led the mountain warriors in the battle?'

'Mwambu, of course! It was Mwambu who led the assault and the onslaught. It was Mwambu, a long time after he had killed most of the monsters and driven off the rest till they had fled and gone and drowned themselves in the far away lake at the end of the world. Then he and his sister Sera started the world anew and re-populated the mountain.'

'But if Mwambu and his sister Sera were the only human beings left on earth, old one, after the monsters had devoured everyone else – from where did Mwambu get a wife and Sera a husband in order to re-populate the mountain?'

'There you go again! That's like asking me if the Creator and man his creature came into being at the same time, out of the same hole. And now you want to ask me if Mwambu became Sera's husband! And I must ask you if the Creator could not create a wife for Mwambu and a husband for Sera from dust or from nothing.'

'But, old one, was it also Mwambu who...'

The bus conductor, who came round to every passenger asking to check his travel ticket, terminated Mwambu's reverie.

Looking out of the window, Mwambu realised that the bus was at that very moment approaching Tororo town, and there to his left beyond the town, rising rigidly to the sky was Tororo Rock, a picaresque volcanic plug, which he had occasionally seen from one hill-top or another in Elgonton district. It now looked to him like a mere dwarfish imitation of Masaaba's mountain, whose peak was often covered by a resplendent cloud of the Creator's presence.

But now he silently wondered as to how it was that from that close distance, the cylindrical plug, with its cleft top, weirdly looked like the male organ. It seemed as if some up-facing subterranean giant was invisibly inseminating the feminine sky and impregnating it with a myriad invisible spirits, good or malignant. And he remembered how Hare, in the often retold fireside tale, craftily disguised his phallic tail as a mushroom and advised his widowed young mother-in-law, whom he was secretly lusting for, that if she wanted another baby, she should go squat and gyrate upon a certain mushroom that she would find sprouting through a hole on a certain anthill, and he dashed ahead of her to go and become that mushroom, so that...

'Attention, fellow travellers,' the bus conductor called, once again interrupting Mwambu's fantasy, as the bus was pulling to a stop on the side of the road some three miles after Tororo. 'This is to allow you to get out and stretch your legs. We shall not stop again until we reach Jinja town.'

Mwambu was impressed by the conductor's pleasant euphemism. So he got out to perform what most passengers were busy doing along the edge of the thicket – which Elgonton Secondary School students called 'watering the grass', or 'conducting a titration exercise'. And at that very instant he recalled with a wry smile the character somewhere in Jonathan Swift's writings who is described by the author as excusing himself from his fellow travellers and going behind a tree 'to obey the exigencies of nature'.

* * *

For the first time since departing from Elgonton that morning, Mwambu looked back during the temporary opportunity of leaving the bus. His attention was instantly arrested by the distorted spectacular shape of Masaaba's Mountain, now on the distant eastern horizon, resembling some massive prehistoric lion lying down, with its head facing north, its raised posterior to the south, and its tapering tail stretching far into what one passenger said was the western end of neighbouring Kenya Colony.

With that view of the disproportionately elevated posterior of the mountain, Mwambu's thoughts hopped off into the world of giants once more as he returned to the bus and the journey resumed. Maybe, he figured, Masaaba's Mountain was a sleeping giant for real, which would one day suddenly get up on all its fours and begin roaring and prowling about the endless world in fantastic style. Ah, what a supreme spectacle that would be! And as he thought of gigantic mythical beings, he recalled the recitation about big things that he had been made to memorise at Namwombe Primary School:

> If all the men in the world were one man,
> And all the axes in the world were one axe,
> And all the trees in the world were one tree,
> And all the rivers in the world were one river,
>
> And if that man took that axe and cut that tree
> And if that great tree fell into that great river –
>
> What a great splash that would be!

But maybe every mountain was a major giant, he told himself, and every hill a minor giant. For in one of the unforgettable tales that his mother had told him in the fireside years there was that Monster whom Hunchback once mistook for a nearby hill in the dark, on which there were two serrated rows of burning coals. Because fire had died out in his homestead, Hunchback walked across with an axe and started smiting one of the coals upon the hillside for a splinter of fire to take to his home. At each stroke of the axe, Monster mumbled something in his sleep about some slight pain in one of his exposed teeth! "I wonder what the problem is with this smallest tooth of mine,' complained Monster to himself without opening his eyes. Oh how Hunchback panicked and fled for dear life upon discovering that he had been hacking away at a giant's tooth! Yes, maybe every mountain, Mwambu concluded, every hill and every valley was a sleeping giant or dwarf or even –

The abrupt entry of the bus into Busitema Forest jolted him back to the geographical reality of his present surroundings. A short while afterwards, the bus emerged from the narrow forest onto an immense plain of lush grasslands and broad, sluggish rivers.

Towards noonday, at a small township on a gentle rise upon the extensive plain, the bus slowed down and turned right into a petrol station to refuel. Momentarily losing his sense of direction under the overhead sun, Mwambu shut and reopened his eyes and told himself that Kampala was to his left and Elgonton to his right.

After quickly topping up its tank, the bus swung at right angles back into the road. At that very moment, Mwambu caught a quick glimpse of the eastern horizon beneath the cloudless sky.

'Where has the mountain gone?' he whispered to himself in visible panic and loud enough for his neighbour to hear.

'What?' curiously returned the elderly man in a white kanzu, the tunic of Islamic origin that, with secular modifications, was fast gaining the status of a Ugandan traditional dress for men. 'What did you say about mountains?'

'Where has it gone?' Mwambu repeated, more to himself than to his elderly neighbour.

'You mean the mountain in the east?' smiled the neighbour. 'Oh, you can't see it from here – because it is now beyond the horizon.'

'What!' Mwambu exhaled as if the bottom had fallen out of him. '*Beyond* the horizon?'

'Yes,' said the neighbour reassuringly, 'You're too far to see it from here.'

Ah, but how could he Mwambu tell that to the child in his inside? How could he tell him that there was now nothing holding up the heavens along the horizon, or that the invisible central pillar rising to the dome of the sky from his father's homestead had never been there? No, he could not tell him that! 'No, I can't!' he involuntarily whispered to himself.

'You can't what?' asked the neighbour, turning and looking piercingly at Mwambu.

'Oh, it's nothing,' he half lied as he tried to hide his embarrassment of having been caught thinking aloud.

'Nothing?' asked the probing fellow passenger.

'Yes, sir – I mean, yes, old one,' Mwambu respectfully replied.

'My name is Muntu,' said the elderly man.

'Oh, really!' exclaimed Mwambu, directly looking into his neighbour's eyes for the first time since boarding the bus at Elgonton.

Muntu was amused by the young man's apparent curious naivety.

'Yes, really,' he amiably replied, as Mwambu fantastically mixed up the speaker with the legendary Mundu – the first man to emerge into existence from a hole on Masaaba's mountain.

'Sir,' Mwambu started to say, when something ahead of him on the road suddenly took away all his attention. 'S-s-sir-,' he stammered, 'are you seeing what I am seeing on the road?'

'Maybe I am,' Muntu calmly answered. 'What are *you* seeing?'

'I seem to be seeing a pool of water on the road, but as we approach it, it shifts to another depression further ahead!'

'Ah,' remarked Muntu. 'It must be your first journey on a tarmac road on a hot afternoon?'

'Yes,' Mwambu anxiously conceded.

'Well,' explained Muntu, 'there's no water on the road at all. What you are seeing is a falsehood, a deception of the eyes. It is patches of the sky that are briefly mirrored in the heated tarmac. Young man, have you never heard of mirages?'

'Yes, yes,' Mwambu fumblingly replied. 'But I thought that they only happen in deserts – such as the Sahara or the Kalahari.'

'Well,' Muntu teased, 'it depends on what you understand by the word "desert". If it's a place where no trees and grass grow, then don't you think that the tarmac road is a desert?'

'Y-e-s – in a way,' Mwambu wonderingly nodded. He fleetingly remembered his Geography teacher at Elgonton saying that the Antarctica continent, around the earth's southern pole, was all covered by ice and was therefore a desert.

In the increasing afternoon heat he started getting used to the mirages, as in progression the bus crossed streams, rivers and swamps of flat countryside. Then at the top of one hill in mid-afternoon, a fantastic new spectacle sprang into view.

'Look, look!' cried Mwambu, gripping Muntu's arm and pointing through the window. 'Don't tell me that *that* over there is another falsehood or trickery of the eyes!'

'No,' answered Muntu with a kind patronising smile. 'You would need a million times a million times a million mirages to produce that one. That is Nalubaale. What the pink men call Lake Victoria.'

'Ah, Nalubaale that soon!' marvelled Mwambu. Whatever its name: whether Nalubaale or Nabuloolo, as the people of Elgonton knew it to be, or Victoria, as named by the red-white men after their queen who ruled their country at the time of 'Europe's carnivorous scramble for Africa', as his History teacher had once put it – or whatever its other names might be – here at last was the child's lake of long, long ago at the far, faraway end of the world.

'And that over there, beginning to appear,' announced Muntu, 'is Jinja town – close to the womb of River Nile, the River of Rivers, and the dungeon of the god of lightning.

* * *

On reaching the bridge on the River of Rivers, the bus pulled up behind a number of vehicles, which were awaiting clearance before crossing over. The passengers got out of the bus and walked around, talking and marvelling at the cranes, tractors and tippers busily moving loads of earth, rocks and metal that were part of some heavy construction work that was going on.

Mesmerised, Mwambu wandered off to the edge of the water. He experienced a deep, thrilling sensation as he bent and touched the clear, sparkling water with his hand, and then with both hands. This was not a million mirages, such as Muntu could have meant, but a real,

43

mighty and flowing expanse of living water. He had seen lake water before, for sure, up on the sky-tall mountain of Masaaba, but it was trapped, stagnant water in a crater pot, so it seemed, for assuaging the thirst of the Creator himself. Here, by contrast, was a confluence of teeming waters on the plains where all mountain streams end: a magnificent reservoir from which the fabulous River of Rivers impatiently gushes forth, tumbles and cascades down, waterfall after waterfall, cataract after cataract, to go sluggishly meander upon and abundantly nourish desert lands so very, very far away that –

In his mind he magically became a child again, on his first day in school long ago stopping in the middle of the stream to let his father wash his legs for him and he following the gurgling stream down, down, down to the world's edge until he felt himself suddenly falling down a sudden cliff to a measureless blankness which so terrified him that he came fleeing back to his father and gripped his shoulders for a firm hold in a real, physical world as he put the other foot forward to be washed and then –

'Passengers of Elgonton-Kampala bus,' shouted the conductor, recalling Mwambu from wonderland, 'go back to your seats and let us get on with our journey.'

'I saw you bowing in obeisance to Nalubaale, goddess of the lake,' remarked Muntu with an enigmatic smile as Mwambu sat down.

'Did I?' asked Mwambu, surprised.

'Yes, you did,' Muntu asserted. 'You should have seen yourself so fondly stroking her exterior, her watery garment, with both hands in an obvious act of worship.'

'Then I did more,' Mwambu fumblingly said, 'than I knew I was doing.' *What a curious man this Muntu is,* he thought. He seemed to know something about everything, from mirages to the spirits that inhabit lake waters.

'Sir, are you –' he started to say but Muntu interrupted him.

'Young man, I have told you my name – what is yours?'

'They call me Mwambu son of Masaaba.'

'Well, then, Mwambu, do you know about the astonishing construction work which is taking place around here?' They were at that moment half way across the twin road and rail bridge.

'Yes, I think I do,' Mwambu replied. 'It is a big, big dam.'

'That's right,' Muntu concurred. 'The pink men are erecting a magical dungeon in which they will conjure the waters of the goddess Nalubaale into permanent lightning. The lightning will then be squeezed into large wires to run across the country and supply it with constant sparks and fatal shocks by day and night through all the seasons.'

Mwambu mused about the incredible notion of conjuring Nalubaale into lightning. Yes, he had known as a child that lightning comes with rain from above in wings of a white cock but returns to the sky as the rain evaporates back. Or did the same Creator 'who inhabits the heights of eternity' – as he remembered reading somewhere – and who touches the world upon mountain peaks, did he also perhaps store his energies in the valleys and hollows of the earth, in the waters of ponds and wells and springs and fountains and oases and creeks and brooks and streams and rivulets and rivers and lakes and seas and oceans and whatever other reservoirs of water that are to be found on earth? Did that same Creator also mould –?

The Forest of Forests, Mabira Forest, came into sudden view as the bus levelled up on a hill half an hour after crossing the River of Rivers. And into the Forest of Forests drove the bus, and seemed to Mwambu like it was snaking its way into the rear and on into the entrails of a massive, imposing and awesome prehistoric living presence: endless squads of huge and exalted tree trunks with extensive deciduous canopies of the greenest green, gigantic creepers up some of those tree trunks, and impenetrable lush undergrowth – all of which cinematically appeared to be running away from the bus backwards into the past where Mwambu was coming from, while the bus sped forward in the opposite direction into the future where he was facing! A sense of the supernatural enveloped him and kept him serenely silent throughout the entire stretch of the forest.

Another half an hour on – that seemed like an eternity to Mwambu – and the bus emerged from the overwhelming immensity of the forest. The terrain that succeeded the forest was dotted with hills and ridges characterised by treeless grassy tops and wooded slopes that ended in broad valleys of papyrus swamps.

'I have to disembark here,' Muntu abruptly announced at some bus stop, recalling Mwambu's mind from far, far away. Instantly Mwambu's inside went hollow, as Muntu had become an indispensable guide on the westward journey.

'If you ever desire me to be your companion on life's road again,' Muntu added as he rose to exit, 'ask for me at the shrine of *Katonda we Butonda* – at the shrine of God of Creation Place.'

At the shrine of Katonda we Butonda... Mwambu intoned to himself, while Muntu jumped off the bus and started walking in the direction from which they had come. *At the shrine of the Creator of Creation Place! That is the spot where creation takes place!* He imagined what an awesome spot that must be! And he decided there and then that one day he would sure go in search of Muntu and that shrine – *the spot where creation takes place ... the spot where creation takes place...*

V
Where Knowledge is the Chief Thing

As the bus eventually laboured its way to its destination, Mr. Bentley's angry parting words sprung to the fore of Mwambu's brain.

Off you go, you scam! And permanent curses upon you if you dare to open that envelope and read its contents! It's not addressed to you, you rogue, you miscreant, you nincompoop, you scoundrel, do you h-e-a-r?

Since collecting his testimonial a month back, he had every passing day barely resisted the temptation to open the envelope and read those forbidden contents. For one thing, Mr. Bentley had signed across the back of the sealed envelope, and the addressee would tell if it had been tampered with before reaching him. And what if he opened it only to find a very devastating testimonial? What would he do about it? Tear it up and go back home? No. So he most unwillingly opted not to open it, but promised himself to one day find out what that fulminating Mr. Bentley of uncouth swear words had written about him. And then, if the contents turned out to be ugly, he would find his way back to the old school and present the red-brown man with an abominable gift he would never forget.

* * *

The inscription on the massive main gate to the university campus dauntingly said: *Pro Futuro Aedificamus*. Mwambu tried to puzzle out the strange words. Not English words, he felt – were they perhaps words from some other colonial European language? Were they French, Spanish, Portuguese, or German?

Or were they from an even more antique language like Greek or Hebrew or whatever was spoken in Egypt of long, long ago?

Above the exotic words were depictions of a giraffe, a crested a crane, a lion and a sailing boat. The odd assortment of land creatures and boat seemed like sentries at the entrance to the fabulous hilltop of his exalted dreams, where he saw himself as going to wage a heroic protracted bloody war against Monster Ignorance.

*   *   *   *   *

The following morning, he knocked on the door of the secretary to the College Registrar and heard a female voice say, 'Come in.'

'Good morning to you,' the voice of the secretary greeted him in a matter-of- fact tone.

'Good morning,' he replied, closing the door behind him. He quickly figured that the elderly pink-skinned lady in a floral pink dress seated upright at the far table near the window with a type-writer in front of her must be the secretary, and that the elderly black man in white short sleeves at the nearer table bowed over a pile of files must be some kind of clerical assistant.

'What can we do for you?' routinely asked the lady.

'I'm a new student and I have a letter here, a testimonial about me. May I please hand it in to you?'

'Yes, over here,' the lady directed, indicating a spot on her table.

Mwambu turned back to head for the door but she asked him to wait for a moment. It was her custom to open a testimonial while the relevant student was still around. Slitting the envelope open with an ivory letter-opener, she took out the testimonial and opened it. And instantly her lower jaw unhinged in utter surprise at what she was seeing.

'Do you call this a testimonial?' she asked, critically narrowing her eyes at Mwambu.

'I, I h-hope so,' was his confused reply. "Or is it not?'

'Of course it's not!' she blurted, magisterially getting up and un-creasing her dress around her generous girth. 'Come with me in to the Registrar.'

She pushed the inner door open, and Mwambu dreamily walked in behind her.

'Mr. Robinson,' she called, placing both the envelope and its contents on the table, 'you have seen all sorts of testimonials and reference letters, but here is one with a difference!' She then quietly left the room, with an ambiguous grin playing on her lips.

A well-groomed gentleman in his prime, attired in a striped light blue shirt with matching navy blue tie, Mr. Robinson was the embodiment of the academic life of the college. In ironic honour to him, the examinations season was popularly known as Robinson Dance. He glanced at the contents of the envelope and gave a wry smile.

'Mr. Mwambu,' he said coolly, 'I know that this is supposed to be a confidential document. But did your former headmaster give you any hint about what he had written about you?'

'No, sir,' he replied, feeling completely at a loss.

'Well, I must tell you that there's no testimonial at all,' Mr. Robinson revealed.

'What!' exclaimed Mwambu. 'What's on that paper, sir?

'Nothing.'

'*Nothing?*'

'Yes, young man, nothing. Or I should more accurately say: it's headed paper bearing the address of your former school (Elgonton Secondary School), date, reference number, subject as 'Testimonial for Abraham Mwambu' underlined – and then *nothing* follows, except for the headmaster's signature (Arthur Bentley) at the very bottom!'

'O no!' Mwambu exhaled. He momentarily closed his eyes and saw a mass of fireflies flickering in the immense darkness before him.

'It's a blank, not a testimonial,' explained Mr. Robinson. 'As we would say in England, it is some kind of weird practical joke by Mr. Bentley. But take it easy, Mr. Mwambu. Perhaps Mr. Bentley has been writing testimonials for so long that he has run short of what to say'

'That may well be the case, sir,' Mwambu managed to say, grateful that the Registrar did not sound as harsh as he might.

'Or, alternatively,' Mr. Robinson amiably continued, 'it may be that Mr. Bentley normally has the basic information typed out on the headed paper, and the actual respective testimonial is typed in later; and that in your case he absentmindedly forgot about the testimonial. Consequently, you have neither a good nor a bad testimonial. And it does not seem to be exactly your fault – on the face of it. I'll write to Mr. Bentley to fill in the blank. I'm aware, of course that testimonials only help in marginal cases. In your case, you have excellent marks in your Cambridge School Certificate Examinations.

'Nevertheless, you have an *unknown*, which is your conduct, your character. But you have my permission to register as a student of this college. All the same, I will keep an eye on you, before and after I hear from Mr. Bentley, as my special case of *a student with a blank.* It's up to you as to what happens to that blank during your stay on this campus. Good day, and good luck, Mr. Mwambu.'

'Thank you, sir,' breathed Mwambu, feeling infinitely relieved, and at the same time utterly unsure how to take what he had just been through since entering the Registrar's office. How was he to take all this? *The unknown is your conduct, your character...you are my special case of a student with a blank...student with a blank...*

*   *   *

On the day of swearing in the fresh entrants, the College Principal and the Registrar walked into the main hall dressed in their colourful academic regalia. The students sprung to their feet. They then sat down to listen to the perennial preliminaries that every incoming lot of students was always subjected to.

'And now stand up again,' pronounced the Registrar, after the Principal had read his written speech and resumed his seat.

The new entrants stood up.

'Everyone please raise your right hand and repeat after me:'

Every right hand went up.

'I solemnly swear before the Principal –'

'I solemnly swear before the Principal'

'That in my stay at Makerere University College –'

'That in my stay at Makerere University College'

'I will diligently seek the *truth* –'

'I will diligently seek the *truth*'

'And nothing but the *truth* –'

'And nothing but the *truth*'

'And because *knowledge* is the chief thing –'

'And because *knowledge* is the chief thing'

'I will acquire my *utmost* of it –'

'I will acquire my *utmost* of it'

'Therewithal also gain *understanding* –'

'Therewithal also gain *understanding*'

'And that I will do this in the spirit of *disinterested* pursuit of knowledge –'

'And that I will do this in the spirit of *disinterested* pursuit of knowledge'

'That is to say, not with a *utilitarian* perspective on knowledge –'

'That is to say, not with a *utilitarian* perspective on knowledge'

'Fully aware that knowledge by its very nature is *useful* –'

'Fully aware that knowledge by its very nature is *useful*'

'And that knowledge is *power*! – '

'And that knowledge is *power*!'

'So help me God –'

'So help me God.'

*   *   *

*And that knowledge is power... that knowledge is power... that knowledge is power...*The words kept ringing deep down in Mwambu's inside as he and fellow fresh students left the main hall. *That knowledge is power...that knowledge is power...that knowledge is power... What else is power...? Politics is power... the white man is power... the platform is power... the pulpit is power... and power is truth... truth is power... knowledge is power...knowledge is power...*

*   *   *

As he emerged through the outer door from the swearing-in ceremony, jostled by his fellow inductees, a final year Education Diploma student he had met the previous day slapped Mwambu on the shoulder. 'Hey, man, what are you thinking and mumbling about?'

'Oh, nothing in particular,' he replied, brightening up. 'Or perhaps I should say,' he continued half-seriously, 'that like everyone else coming from the swearing-in must be doing, I'm thinking about *seeking the truth!*'

'Come on, don't be daft!' was the jovial reply, as the two walked on in the direction of the chapels. 'Seeking the truth is not as big a thing as you might be imagining.'

By the end of the first week, Mwambu discovered that the term had long established itself as the most cynical idiom on the campus. Idle students loitering on the grass would dismissively laugh off a fellow student gravitating towards the lecture room or library by remarking that he was hurrying to go seek the truth. A frequenter of the Guild Canteen would jokingly declare, as he emptied bottle after bottle of his favourite intoxicant, that he was tuning himself up for seeking the truth. And an adventurous young man who sneaked into the women's quarters after official visiting hours would later proudly inform his cronies how he had the previous night sought the truth in 'The Box' – meaning the women's original wooden habitation that stood on concrete stilts just a stone throw from the main gate.

'By the way,' continued the final year student, 'I didn't catch your name yesterday.'

'I'm called Mwambu Masaaba.'

'Ah, you're M x M! And I'm sure that's a name from the mountain where the sun comes from,' remarked the final year student.

'That's correct. And what's yours? '

'They call me Michael Musisi – or simply M²'

'I have heard about you! You're the President of the Makerere Political Club?'

'That's right.'

'Musisi is a name from the plains around here, isn't it?'

'You're dead right,' was the jovial reply. 'So right now, you can say that the Mountain is talking to the Plains!'

How very interesting that he should say that, Mwambu thought to himself. 'What does your name mean, if I may ask?'

'It's the name of the god of earthquakes. You see, I am a god!'

'Wow!' exclaimed Mwambu, enchanted like a little child. 'You're a god and also president of a student club?'

'Yes,' Musisi playfully answered. 'I am a political god.'

'That's a superb combination of heaven and earth,' remarked Mwambu, catching up with Musisi's flight of mind.

'You'll be most welcome,' Musisi continued, 'to the meetings of Makerere Political Club. They take place every first Saturday of the month in the annex to the Guild office at 5.00 o'clock in the evening. Would you be interested?'

'For sure, for sure!' Mwambu enthused. And he carried on in an enchanted mode, 'Can I be there as priest and prophet to the political god?'

'Ah, that may have to be decided,' Musisi cautioned, 'by the triumvirate of the resident gods. For I must reveal to you that on this very hill I have my two brother gods –'

'What!' Mwambu was mesmerised.

'Yes. And they also happen to be my *year-mates* as well as my *course-mates* and *cause-mates*. They are called Methuselah Musoke and Moses Mukasa.'

'And what makes them gods?' Mwambu asked in wonderment.

They were just then passing under a gigantic mango tree planted a long time back, by one of Makerere's pioneer combined bearer of Britain's Union Jack and the Cross, to stand at equal distances between the two chapels, one for the Catholics and the other for the Protestants. Mwambu was taking a fast liking to this compelling senior student. Musisi made a gesture in the direction of the permanent concrete bench under the mango tree and they sat on it.

'What makes them gods, is that your question?'

'Yes, that's my question.'

'Well, it's simply that they *are* gods,' Musisi answered matter-of-factly. 'Musoke is the god of the rainbow, and Mukasa is the god of the sea and all waters. Does that satisfy your curiosity?'

'No, it does not,' Mwambu replied. 'Are you saying that you and they are gods or that you bear the names of gods?'

'Same thing,' pronounced Musisi. 'We're gods because we bear those names; and we bear those names because we're gods.'

'And how come,' Mwambu inquisitively pried, sensing an uncanny affinity on account of his own name that Musisi had just reduced to M x M, 'that the names of the three of you all start with M? That's to say, both your family and adopted names, as I should call them.'

' M is for "masculine",' replied Musisi on the spur of the moment, though knowing very well as he did that there were also gods whose names did not start with the same letter – Katonda, Kiwanuka, Lubaale and a host of others.

'And N is for "non-masculine",' Musisi animatedly carried on, '– for the wives and daughters of gods: such as Namusisi, Namusoke, Namukasa.'

Mwambu was entranced, but at the same time started feeling that he was being sucked into some weird magic whirlpool. He wondered if he was not dreaming, if this conversation was not taking place while he was fast asleep perhaps somewhere back home in his mountain land and he had not yet arrived at Makerere. But maybe he was awake, and this just a most unexpected encounter so soon after the swearing-in ceremony. 'Is that orange and yellow sun on the low horizon rising or setting?' he asked himself by way of checking if he was sane and sober.

'You say that people call you M²,' Mwambu drowsily resumed. 'How about Musoke and Mukasa – are they also M²?'

'No, they're not. Musoke is popularly known as MM and Mukasa as 2M.'

'But if you're almighty gods,' Mwambu called out, closely peering into Musisi's eyes, 'what are you doing at Makerere and what are you doing with those Bible names – Michael, Methuselah and Moses?'

'That's part of the game!' Musisi declared. 'Michael, according to your Bible-lore, is commander of heaven's army; Methuselah the man that lived longest; Moses the greatest initiator of the law in the Northern hemisphere. We three embody what those three names signify in our own, rival sphere.'

'Is that why you chose to be baptised gods?' Mwambu quizzed.

Musisi shot up onto his feet as though stung by a scorpion. Mwambu also stood up, screwing his eyes upon Musisi.

'No, you can't baptise a god!' protested Musisi, austerely darting his eyes around the mango tree. 'We weren't baptised when we acquired those names. We bought them.'

'What!'

'Yes! And we had fake baptism certificates written out.'

'You bought the names?' Mwambu could not believe the senselessness of what he was hearing. 'From who, for how much, and what for did you buy them?'

'From one drunken Reverend Father, one greedy Fathering Reverend, and one gullible Catechist.'

'For how *much*?'

'I M² provided one bottle of *waragi* (crude gin) mixed with goat urine for the Reverend Father; MM made available a youthful woman with chronic venereal infection as extra-marital mistress for the Fathering Reverend; and 2M supplied a pregnant pig that had been mounted by a dog for the Catechist.'

'Impossible!' Mwambu's voice rang out.

'But true,' calmly replied Musisi. 'That's how we acquired our exotic names – what you call "adopted" names – and got away with them without ever having entered church even once up to now.'

'For what purpose? And do you mean to say that you escaped going to missionary schools?'

'Precisely! We attended Moslem schools throughout; and there we had it generally believed wrongly that we had converted to Islam. And for convenience, we went by the names of Muhammad, Musa, and Mustapha. As for what cause, or what purpose, you will learn in due course if we continue to meet.'

Mwambu was mystified.

'So are you men, gods or ghosts?'

'That's our secret!' replied Musisi with an enigmatic smile. 'You will find out *later than sooner*. Last year under this very tree, which we call the Equidistant Tree, we the Triumvirate met and decreed that in not more than twelve revolutions of the Earth round the Sun from thence, this land must come under the influence of an unprecedented radical phenomenon. You should live to see what it will be. Will you be there?'

Mwambu was lost for an answer.

'God willing,' he managed to say. And then he added dubiously, 'Or should I say if the Triumvirate gods are willing?'

As though he thought Mwambu's question did not need an answer, Musisi walked away without another word. He walked away into the twilight.

Rubbing his eyes like one waking from sleep, Mwambu turned and walked in the opposite direction towards his hall of residence, now massively silhouetted against the twilight sky.

* * *

A freshmen's dance in the Main Hall as usual launched the academic year in rhythmic style. A second year student by the name of Stanley Lwanga, in the same hall of residence as Mwambu, informed him that for every such occasion as well as end-of-year parties a live band was always in attendance.

'What's more,' Lwanga revealed, 'extra dance partners are always imported from The Zoo and The Library.'

'And what places on earth are those?' Mwambu asked, puzzled.

'Ah, you haven't picked up that one yet,' Lwanga observed.

'No. I know about the university library, but how can a zoo supply dance partners?'

'These are terms with a special meaning,' Lwanga explained. 'In Makerere jargon, The Zoo stands for the Nurses' Training College run by the Government. And The Library stands for the Midwives' Training College run by the Church.'

'I see,' said Mwambu. 'But what do Zoos and Libraries have in common?'

'Variety of course!' pronounced Lwanga.

'Ah ha,' Mwambu nodded with a grin.

'And variety,' concluded Lwanga, 'is what the university's own Box of a mere handful of Boxers cannot boast of.'

Tucked away in a cozy corner of the Main Hall, Mwambu and Lwanga, who were fast becoming close friends, sat sipping bottles of beer while the live band blared its favourite tunes. It was a group called the Equator Boys Band that was on stage. They played mostly rumba, tango and twist numbers, familiar enough to excite the male students into a scramble for dance partners. After several numbers there came a popular, lively cha-cha-cha that called upon all age groups to get up and dance –

Everybody cha-cha-cha---a
Every dancer cha-cha-cha---a
Every lover cha-cha-cha---a
Equator Boys cha-cha-cha---a

Immediately following upon that expression of general happiness, which saw almost everybody take to the floor, the Entertainment Minister also doubling as Master of Ceremonies, went up to the microphone.

'Ladies and gentlemen,' he called out, 'I'm told that the next number will be a waltz. Let me request, for the sake of fairness, that this time it's the fair sex to pick their partners.'

There was loud applause from the men, while the band struck the opening notes of the hit number of the year, *Pain and Joy*, whose refrain was:

When the pain in his heart
Is the girl in your arms –

Suddenly, a female shadow fell across Mwambu's crossed legs. He looked up and his eyes met those of the origin of the shadow, now curtseying to him with a naughty smile.

'Oh, um...at your service!' he mumbled.

He rose to his feet and followed his challenger to the centre of the dancing area, praying that he would manage to execute the exacting waltz steps. She instantly struck him as possessing a lovely brown-skinned oval face and a remarkable figure in a shiny dark dress with matching high-heeled black shoes. By the time the waltz was over, he had learnt that she was Nakintu from the Nurses' Training College run by the Government. And she had learnt that he was Mwambu in his preliminary year of studies. And he had asked her if he could look her up at her hostel one day, and she had coyly said that she would not be too surprised to see him.

And then as he was returning her to her seat – was that an apparition that his eyes suddenly fell upon?

Being led by another male student to the seat next to Nakintu's was none other than Nambozo, his former girlfriend at high school, whom he had sworn never to meet again in this world.

He quickly bowed his thank-you to Nakintu and moved like a zombie to go rejoin his friend Lwanga. Over the next hour he sipped continuously from his unfermented bottle between absent-minded scraps of conversation. He was glad when the dance eventually wound up and he headed back to his hall.

VI
In Cupid's Dominion

Mwambu and Lwanga shared not only the same hall of residence, Lord Lugard Hall, named in permanent commemoration of one of Uganda's pioneer colonisers, but many other curricular and non-curricular interests. In their leisure time, they shared childhood and adolescent memories as well as their dreams of the future. For his part, Mwambu was particularly keen to learn the similarities and differences between the pastimes and practices of the young among the people of the plains in comparison to those of his mountain people.

'And so how old were you,' Mwambu one day playfully asked Lwanga, 'when you had your first girlfriend?'

'About five years, I think,' replied Lwanga with a straight face.

'Five years! And your little girlfriend must have been about four years?'

'No, she was not that small. She was a married woman with three children older than me.'

'Wow!' exclaimed Mwambu. 'And how did you know that she was your girlfriend?'

'You see,' Lwanga explained, 'she was and still is the wife of my mother's older brother. We children used to call him Uncle Visitor whenever he came to our home. And we called her Aunt Visitor.'

'And then?' Mwambu was getting really intrigued. 'And then what happened between you and Aunt Visitor?'

'Whenever Uncle Visitor and Aunt Visitor came to visit us, we were all so happy to see them just as they were so happy to see us. Uncle Visitor would hug me and fondly call me his dear nephew. Aunt Visitor would also fondly hug me. But instead of calling me her nephew, she called me her dear man! "*Mwami wange*, my husband" she would say. The first time she called me this, in the presence of my parents and Uncle Visitor, I scratched my little head and asked my mother if Aunt Visitor was my wife. "Yes, she is your wife," chorused my mother, father and Uncle Visitor! "Yes, I am your wife," Aunt Visitor added by herself, beaming at me! So from that day on I knew that I had a girlfriend – in fact, a wife. It was only as I grew older that I learnt that among my people, all the wives of a mother's brothers and cousins are one's wives. One can fondle them, in public as well as in private. One can even share a bed with them – one at a time, of course!'

'Incredible! Incredible!' was Mwambu's more than surprised rejoinder. 'Up where I come from, your mother's brother's wife is like your wife's mother – untouchable. For us, your mother's brother is like your *male mother*. So his wife is like your own mother.'

'Well, that's you, and this is us,' Lwanga observed, wearing an old man's wise look. 'And if I may turn the tables against you,' he continued with a half grin, 'were you also five when you had your first girlfriend?'

'No, no, I wasn't as precocious as you! I was seven.'

'And who was the experimental little one?'

'Not a little one. Not even a human being. It was a tree,' Mwambu revealed.

'A tree! You're crazy, Mwambu!'

'Well, not quite a tree,' he calmly went on. 'It was a shrub. It's what the pink men call 'aloe vera'. The plant grows wild in our hills and around the homesteads. So when I was about seven, I saw that the bigger boys, as they herded their parents' cattle, would take off time to derive secret fun from the thick and fleshy leaves, or rather limbs, of the aloe vera plant. They would each split one leaf open down the middle with their bare hands – then proceed to rub their stiff little members upon the opened-up leaf, pretending that they were lying with a woman. So you can guess as to who was my first girlfriend or woman!'

'No!' protested Lwanga, shutting his eyes and slapping his hands upon his ears. 'No, I don't want to guess!'

'But I'm sure you have already guessed rightly,' Mwambu teased.

'Maybe I have, maybe I haven't,' Lwanga uneasily replied, fighting with his imagination. 'And what do you call that plant up there, if I may ask?'

'Ah, depending on what part of the mountain you grow up on –

>It's li-tyakatyaka
>
>Or li-tyeketyeke
>
>Or li-tyikityiki
>
>Or li-tyokotyoko
>
>Or li-tyukutyuku
>
>Or li-tyaketyoku

Between them, as you may learn one day, these variations of the name for this plant exhaust all the five vowel sounds of the language of the people of the Sunrise Mountain.'

'I think you're scandalous, Mwambu,' Lwanga cheerfully commented.

'And I think, you're incredulous, Lwanga,' Mwambu reciprocated as warmly.

*   *   *

After their first meeting on the university dance floor, it took a whole year of repeated invitations before Nakintu was persuaded to pay Mwambu a visit in his room in Lord Lugard Hall. She arrived on the stroke of six in the evening, which was the time she had promised to come over, and Mwambu figured that she must be a really disciplined person. She was clad in a light blue floral dress and navy blue flat shoes, while her host was in white short sleeves with sky blue stripes, dark grey trousers and black sandals.

Mwambu tried his best to hide his excitement on seeing his first-time, hard-won visitor. Closing the door behind her, he showed her to the chair at his reading desk, which he had arranged to face inwards, and then sat himself on the bed directly across from the chair.

'My, you can keep time!' he complimented her, after formally shaking hands.

'Yes, I have to,' she cheerfully answered. 'Otherwise you wouldn't know that I went to the right school – what everybody knows as *the* school.'

'Ah, you sure went to *the* school?' Mwambu asked jovially. 'How come then,' he joked, 'that I didn't see you there?'

'See me where?' she replied, a little puzzled.

'At *the* school – Elgon Secondary School.'

She gave a happy laugh, thereby exposing two rows of pure white teeth, like those of a millet eater.

'By *the* school,' she correctively announced, looking out of the window onto the well-mowed lawn, 'I of course mean Nile Girls' High School. Or are you the *last* person,' she cheekily asked, 'to know that fact?'

'No,' Mwambu countered, 'I may be the *first* to know it!'

They laughed merrily together. Then she quickly placed her hand across her mouth, telling herself that she was giving too much of herself too soon, while he was glad that she seemed to be a really straightforward person.

'Oh, but I'm making you talk on saliva, as we say at home,' Mwambu remarked. 'Please let me offer you a drink.'

'That's OK, thank you,' Nakintu said.

"Which drink please?' He walked across to the reading desk and removed a cloth from the bottles sitting on a tray. 'As you can see, I've got a bit of variety.'

'Water please,' she said, not seeing her preference on the tray.

'What!' Mwambu's eyes dilated in amusement and mild confusion.

'Yes, water please,' she calmly repeated. 'That is, if you have it in stock.'

Of all things, it was not in supply anywhere in the room.

'Distilled,' he enumerated by way of trying to save face, 'mineral, sugared, hot, iced, or in what form?'

'Ordinary clay-pot water. I was brought up on water.'

Mwambu's mind flew back to his childhood days: calling into the water-pot to his mother to come home quickly from wherever she was...going with mother down to the fountain to draw water while the setting sun shone its soft light upon the mountain...clear rain water in the rain puddles which assumed a fantastic mud-brown colour when children danced in it.

'And how come,' he asked, returning to the present, 'that you were brought up on water?'

'It's because my father taught us, children, that water is the best drink in the world, followed by water.'

'Wow! That sounds so good – water followed by water!' Mwambu enthused, returning to the bed.

'We were surrounded by so much fresh water where I grew up. My parents, therefore, decided to bring us up on this free bounty, as sober children, and I have not regretted it.'

'In that case, please permit me to leave the room for a couple of minutes to dash to the hall canteen and return with some "clay-pot" water.'

'No, no, no. Please don't bother. I don't have to have a drink, and I'm not even feeling thirsty. As "man shall not live by bread alone" – so the Bible teaches –,' she naughtily quoted at him, 'neither should woman, I believe, live by drink all along.'

By now Mwambu was beginning to convince himself that he was meeting more than his equal. His school-boyish idea of a woman as being shy and inexpressive on a first date was being given a smart thrashing. He somehow felt that she was ahead of him in some things, in some ways.

'All the same,' he rallied, 'judging by your happy addiction to water, it would seem that it's your natural habitat. Did you grow up on Lake Victoria, or on one of its islands? Was it Buvuma or Ssese islands?'

'On the contrary, I grew up in Mabira Forest. In a cultivated clearing of Mabira.'

'Wonder of wonders!' exclaimed Mwambu.

'What's wonder of wonders about that?' she asked. She was beginning to think that he must be a somehow awkward young man.

'The wonder of wonders,' he replied, 'is that you seem to be made of everything that I do not expect. Should I assume, since you grew up in a forest clearing, that your father is a farmer, or a forester?'

'Neither,' she announced, enjoying her teasing rejoinders to his expectations.

'You see! Your father is not what he might be. What's he, what does he do?'

'He's a priest. He's a Native Anglican Church (NAC) parish priest.'

'There you are!' declared Mwambu somewhat triumphantly, as if gratified to have confirmed a theory. 'Even your father is a surprise. Then I must not ask about your mother, your siblings, and your clan – because I'll get only unexpected answers.'

'Which perhaps means,' she calmly observed, 'that someone can gather information about something by means other than asking questions. For instance, through just making a request for the information that's needed. That's to say, a request which is not in the form of a question.'

And now Mwambu was thinking: *Perhaps she should be training to be a teacher, not a nurse; and I should not be aiming to become a teacher, but something else which I do not yet know.*

'Next time, if there will be a next time,' Nakintu started to say –

'Oh yes,' he interrupted her in visible panic, 'there must be a next time, please!'

'Next time then, as there must be a next time,' she continued, 'I'll without asking questions need to know everything about you, your father, your mother, your siblings, and your clan.'

But for now, she said, she wanted to remark that it had just occurred to her that since he had come from Elgon Secondary School, he should know an old girl of the same school who was currently her classmate at the Nurses' Training College. Maybe she was even his classmate at their school, and he must have seen her at that freshmen's dance earlier in the year.

'Her name is Jane Nambozo,' she said.

Taken completely unawares, Mwambu blinked a couple of times, opened his mouth meaning to say something but nothing came out in good time.

'Y-e-s, I know Nambozo,' he fumbled, aware of Nakintu's eyes keenly fixed on him. Looking out of the window, he repeated in a flat voice, 'Yes, I know Jane Nambozo.'

'I see,' said Nakintu, and he sensed that she meant it in more than one sense. 'I now also remember that when you saw me back to my seat after we danced together, she too was returning to her seat next to mine but you did not seem to recognise each other. Next time,' she pursued, 'maybe you will also like to tell me everything about her as well.'

'No, I won't,' Mwambu replied very firmly, rigidly straitening himself up on the bed and beginning to feel quite offended by this first-time visitor who was behaving like an investigator. 'No, I won't – because I don't know everything about her!'

'OK, then,' Nakintu tried to play it cool. 'I shouldn't have said you tell me everything. Just tell me anything or something about her.'

'I don't know anything or something important about her,' Mwambu irritably replied. 'And that is it,' he flatly announced.

Silence ensued for the next couple of minutes. It was that kind of sudden silence following upon a talkative conversation, during which silence – as children of Mwambu's primary school days used to say – angels wrote down what had just been spoken.

It was Nakintu who broke the silence. 'I think I've seen you enough,' she said, uncrossing her legs and briefly fanning them under the chair. Mwambu understood her to mean that she wanted to leave.

'Not so soon!' he pleasantly protested, coming alive.

'Yes, I think I've seen you enough for one day,' she replied, sounding as amiable as she could. 'I must get back soon.'

'Oh yes,' agreed Mwambu. 'But I had imagined that you were devoting the whole evening to me. Or is baby,' he playfully asked, 'crying at home?'

'What! Which baby?' There was evident shock in her voice. *O God, has some malicious gossip of a woman perhaps revealed to him that... but no, it's impossible!*

He sensed that she did not know the idiomatic saying about one being in an undue hurry as if one was rushing to go breast-feed a crying baby. He had just translated the idiom from his own mother tongue.

'Why do you ask me that question?' she suspiciously demanded, getting onto her feet and wandering to the window.

'Or is baby,' Mwambu pressed on with his joke, 'not at home?'

She swung round and faced him with a ruffled countenance. 'Which home?' she demanded. *Jesus, he doesn't ask if there IS a baby at home, but if it's NOT at home!*

'One or the other,' he went on. 'It can be one's own or another's home.'

'I think I must leave now,' she announced, walking to the door with all the composure she could summon from deep inside her. 'Because I don't know what you're talking about. But it's been very nice visiting you.'

'The same for me,' replied Mwambu without much feeling, getting up from the bed.

He walked to the door to open it for her and to see her off. And as they walked to the bus he wondered what it was that he had said towards the end that had so visibly upset her. He promised himself to be more tactful and less talkative next time.

'If there'll be a next time,' he reminded himself.

* * *

Nakintu was born the third child and first daughter among a total of nine siblings, the only other girl in the family being the last-born. The Reverend Simon Kintu and his wife, Mary, brought up the children as religiously as they best knew how. As they grew up, the children were progressively instructed in all the virtues of the faith of their parents, such as temperance, self-control and purity. And they were as progressively warned against all the vices of the flesh and the spirit, such as rudeness, dishonesty and fornication. Very often, the Reverend quoted at the children his favourite verse from St. Paul's letters – 'Flee youthful pleasures!'

In addition to being the vicar of his parish, North Mabira parish, he was also Chairman of Fathers' Union, while his wife was the Chairwoman of Mothers' Union. The first cardinal point of both Unions was sanctity of the marital bed; and the second cardinal point was self-control and purity among the offspring.

Nevertheless, the flesh being the flesh and the spirit being the spirit, across the many years of active service in the church, the Reverend Kintu was rumoured to have fathered up to seven extra children (one for every day of the week, said his detractors). They were begotten with married and unmarried female parishioners who adored his fiery sermons as well as the energies that he injected into his passionate and compassionate pastoral visits. As for Mary his wife, it was generally known that she had contrived only one extra-marital child, a boy, with the ruffian to whom she had originally so madly wanted to get married but had lost to a more cunning younger woman from his own village.

One chance morning at the very start of the long vacation following the end of Nakintu's second year at Nile Girls' High School, Mary Kintu noticed something ungainly about her daughter. Upon being sternly quizzed, Nakintu confessed that she had not seen the moon for the last six moons.

'Don't tell me that, Sally!' exclaimed her infuriated mother. 'And you only fourteen, not yet even fifteen! My God, my God, how can this be? How, how, how? And why have you forsaken us, O Lord? Why have you forsaken Simon and me your humble handmaid? Why? Why? Why, O Lord?'

To all demands, pleas, threats, coaxing and cajoling by her mother to reveal the father of the pregnancy, Nakintu answered with tight-lipped, stubborn silence. She had sworn to herself that to her dying day, she would never reveal to anybody the identity of the illiterate chicken thief in the village who had enticed her and done this thing to her. He had soon thereafter migrated to a distant part of the country without knowing of Nakintu's pregnancy.

The Reverend and Mrs. Kintu quickly considered all possible alternatives out of the family crisis. They agreed that the good image of the family before the congregation and the general public must be maintained at all costs.

'But abortion is firmly ruled out,' the Reverend pronounced.

'Yes, yes,' his wife concurred. 'Murdering the unborn is the worst kind of murder.'

It was accordingly decided that Nakintu should be taken to the home of her mother's younger sister in Kyaggwe countryside. And this was carried out the very following day, before Nakintu's condition might become obvious to the village gossips that would have found extreme pleasure in discovering what had befallen the Reverend's pious household.

One week after her baby girl was born, Nakintu returned home without the baby. It was not suckled even once by its mother but was instead handed over to the aunt, to adopt and breast-feed alongside her own newborn baby boy.

In that way, Nakintu's aunt became Nnaalongo the mother of twins, for so the neighbours called her; while her husband, a diviner-herbalist very much sought after throughout Kyaggwe, became Ssaalongo Muntu the father of twins, whom Mwambu was to meet by chance on his first journey to the capital city.

And upon her rejoining her parents, her breasts still sprouting, Nakintu resolved to remain as good as a virgin for a long time to come.

VII
Of Kundu and Kintu

After her first visit to Mwambu, weeks later when Nakintu was persuaded to pay her second visit, both host and guest were this time more cautious in their conversation. As soon as the niceties of welcome and exchange of local news were over, Mwambu went quiet.

'How come,' Nakintu teased, 'you're not so talkative today?'

'Because I was too talkative last time,' Mwambu coolly replied. 'And I don't wish to displease you by saying something careless or stupid at the very start.'

'All the same, you promised to tell me about two things in your life.'

'And what are those two things?' Mwambu asked with a slight wrinkling of the face. 'Can you remind me?'

'I'll only remind you,' Nakintu teased again, 'if you have an old man's memory.'

'Yes, it's possible,' Mwambu cheerfully admitted, 'that I have an old man's brain in a young man's body. Please remind me.'

'It was about your family and your past schoolmate who is now my classmate at the Nurses' Training College.'

'Ah well, about my family first. I have a father and a mother by the names of Masaaba and NaBusuulwa; and all my siblings are one sister who comes after me, and whose name is Khalayi.'

'That's a very small family!'

'Yes, it is.'

'And about your former classmate who is now my classmate?'

'She may be the best person to tell you how we used to be friends and why we're no longer so.'

'Yes, she has told me that you chucked her in the last term of the last year of school.'

'On the contrary, she chucked herself,' Mwambu feelingly carried on, 'by becoming the sex accomplice of an old *muzungu* (pink-man) teacher more than twice her age. Did she tell you that? Did she also tell you it was that old hog that ended her virginity in the chapel vestry?'

'What!' Nakintu exclaimed in disbelief. 'Inside a chapel, did you say?'

'Yes, that's what I said.'

'With the congregation watching?'

'No, I didn't say that.'

'Then who saw them?'

'It was one accidental passer-by.'

'And who was that?

'Does it matter who it was?'

'All the same,' Nakintu pressed on, 'how can you be sure it was the *muzungu* who ended her virginity?'

'Oh!' Mwambu was amazed by the question. 'Did she tell you it was someone else that did it?'

'No, she didn't. But suppose it was on an earlier occasion, and by none other than you?'

'Miss Nakintu!' Mwambu exclaimed, scandalised.

'I'm sorry,' Nakintu quickly apologised. 'I'm sorry I've apparently gone too far.'

'Yes, you had better be sorry,' Mwambu told her, getting to his feet and moving to the window. 'Because, madam, I'm not taking away any woman's virginity till my wedding night.'

'Ah, that's very principled of you!' Nakintu uneasily complimented, as she inwardly told herself: *That won't be me, O my God!* 'Can we please change the topic?' she implored.

'Very gladly,' replied Mwambu, returning to his chair. 'Let's change to something nice that I've been meaning to ask you about.'

'And what is that?'

'It's your name. It's a very curious name.'

'In which way is it curious?'

Mwambu stroked his chin like an old wise man might do.

'I'll tell you in the form of a story,' he said. 'A long time ago a young man left his home on the Mountain of the Sun, now renamed Mount Elgon, to go on a fact-finding expedition. After many hazardous days and nights through unmapped trackless jungle, he arrived on the northern shores of Lake Nalubaale. By that time he had lost the way back home. So he decided to stay where he was, to settle in the jungle and to tame it. His original name was Kundu, and he was brother to my great great-grandfather backwards to the *n*th generation.'

'That's interesting,' Nakintu observed.

'His name, Kundu, in my language means "Thing, Object", or more accurately, "Big Thing".'

'Ah, that means the same,' Nakintu remarked in a flash of perception, 'as "Kintu". It means "Thing". Kintu, as you should know, is the grandfather of all my people, the BaGanda.'

'And that's why I find your name to be curious, fascinating – because it's derived from "Kintu".'

'Yes, it is – and so?'

'And so it's like all the other names for girls that I hear all around me –Namatovu, Nabukenya, Namusoke, and so on.'

'That's right,' Nakintu concurred in a neutral tone. 'They're female versions of their male counterparts: Matovu, Bukenya, and Musoke.'

'Eureka! Now I've got it!' Mwambu cheerfully exploded, teasingly looking straight into Nakintu's eyes. 'Your curious name, Nakintu, means "Female-Thing"!'

Nakintu burst into happy, prolonged laughter at his cleverish play with words.

'Yes!' he carried on in the spirited manner of one announcing a great discovery. 'You're Female-Thing, Female-Thing-a-ma-bob, Female-Thing-a-mmy, and Female-what's-its-name!'

'What a whole weird string of made-up words!' And she was thinking, *He has a really crazy brain.*

'And, therefore,' he continued in the same declamatory vein, 'what it comes down to is this. My Kundu is your Kintu. And that Kintu didn't drop ready-made from the sky, as your stories retell, but came walking from the mountain of the farthest east. As a result, you're my relation, my cousin, to the hundredth generation. My blood told me who you are when we first met on the freshmen dance floor. And I thought to myself what a wonderful homecoming it would be if you could someday accompany me to the mountain country. We could call it "Kintu Finds out about Kundu Expedition".'

By now Nakintu was mesmerised by Mwambu's tale of origins, her lips half-parted in wonder.

Suddenly, Mwambu got to his feet, walked to the back of her chair and bent over her, resting his hands on her shoulders.

'Will you come?' he asked from deep down inside him.

'Yes, if you're serious,' Nakintu said, looking sideways and fighting to hold back a flood of untold desire.

'I *am* serious,' Mwambu announced with a trembling voice, stepped to the side and placed himself in front of her. Taking both her hands in his, he pulled her to her feet. In her eyes were teardrops of longing, and in her breast loud beating of accelerated drum-strokes.

'I'm so happy that you'll come!' Mwambu proclaimed, looking into Nakintu's animated face with infinite tenderness.

'And now may I call you my Na-Thing-a-mmy?'

'Yes, you –'

Of all diabolic interruptions in the world, Nakintu's words were cut short by a loud knock on the door.

'Who is there?' Mwambu angrily shouted, while Nakintu hurriedly sat down on the chair and instantly performed the miracle of composing herself to look like a visitor who had just arrived that very minute.

'It's I.'

Mwambu very well knew the voice.

'Don't come in, unless you're the devil!' he irritably called out.

'I *will* come in, as I'm *not* the devil!'

The door opened smartly – and in stepped John Chrysostom Lwanga.

VIII
The Brewing Fifties

One leisurely afternoon after the two of them had become quite well acquainted, Mwambu had told Lwanga about his weird encounter with Michael Musisi the very evening the first year students were sworn in. Mwambu wanted to know what Lwanga thought of a character that claimed he was one of the native gods on the campus, was very active in student politics, and was always at loggerheads with the College administrators. Lwanga explained that there was a strong underground anti-colonial movement on the hill that championed indigenous religions, cultures and traditional political systems. He said that he was himself a supporter of the movement, even though some of its leaders, such as Musisi and his two colleagues with the names of gods might be having some other motives.

Then the day came when the Executive Committee of the Political Club had to hand over the management of the club to the next executive. Musisi stood up to give his prepared brief handover speech.

'My fellow political animals,' he started, partly playful and partly in a sombre mood, 'I salute you all in the name of political consciousness. As I hand over the Presidency of this important club to my successor, I'm gratified in knowing that my executive has throughout the past year maintained among its membership an active awareness of the political climate in our country and around the world.

'I prophesy that this decade will go down in the annals of the history of Uganda and the entire world as "The Brewing Fifties". The year 1947 will be looked back upon by future generations as the year that set the political pace for the rest of the twentieth century. For after India's independence there is no going back.

'This must be the decade in which African and Asian countries must wake up! They must wake up from their slumber of ages, and from the nightmare of the Second World War. They must roundly ask themselves why they became embroiled in a war that was none of their business. How German or British was Africa that her children should take sides in the war of the colonialist, imperialist top dogs? What did Africans and Asians gain from it all? What did their continents have at stake?

'At the beginning of it all, the Caucasians and the Arabs perpetrate the unforgivable evil of slave trade upon Africa. Then the Caucasians squat as famished monsters around a conference table in Berlin at the height of iniquity, in 1884. And, imagining our continent to be a mere carcass, the gluttonous hyenas carve it all up into chunks for themselves. After which they change into the stage costumes of "Global Advancers of the Cross" and "Flag-bearers of Civilisation"!

'I tell you, fellow political animals, that this decade is going to witness the mass exit of those hyenas, those so-called advancers of the cross and Europe's flag-bearers. Yes, the bloody monsters must be hounded out of this continent, sooner than later. Oh yes, Africa and Asia are speedily going to come into their own. They will reinstate their kings and chiefs in all their glory of old, and reinstall their native gods upon their everlasting thrones.

'I'm confident that all of us here are going to be part of that historic change across Africa.'

Looking up from his text and progressively taking in his audience from one end to the other, he asked, 'Who would wish to miss such an opportunity?'

He then abruptly resumed his seat.

Lwanga had previously informed Mwambu that he had expressed an interest in being on the next executive committee of the club, and had persuaded Mwambu to do the same. They were not surprised, therefore, to hear themselves announced as being on the new committee, with Lwanga as the President and Mwambu as a committee member.

* * *

The following morning, a Friday, an office messenger from the office of the College Principal delivered an urgent note to Michael Musisi just as he was leaving his hall of residence to go and attend a lecture. He was required to report to the Principal's office immediately upon the receipt of the note.

And he did exactly that; he reported to the Principal straightaway. The Principal sternly told Musisi that the inflammatory sentiments he had expressed in his hand-over speech the previous day had reached the college administration, and that as the head of that administration, he the Principal was demanding a written apology within the next twenty-four hours. If the apology was not handed in within the specified time, the Principal warned, Musisi should consider himself as suspended from the college for an indefinite period.

'Sir, may I at least ask you,' Musisi said with absolutely unperturbed countenance, 'about the means by which my sentiments, as you call them, reached your ears?'

'That's none of your business,' pronounced the Principal. 'Just you go and write that apology at once, will you?'

'In good time, sir!' answered Musisi.

Biting his lower lip and squinting at the Principal, he turned upon his heels and exited the august office. He instantly resolved on an alternative to the Principal's demand.

Beating the prescribed twenty-four hour deadline, a written communication from Musisi reached the Principal's table. It read:

> UnDear Mr. Principal,
>
> With reference to your demand for an apology for a crime I have not committed, and which you have not proved, this is to inform you that I am denying you the pleasure of receiving such an apology or administering suspension upon me. Instead, I hereby dismiss you from being my principal by discharging myself from your colonialist, imperialist, brainwashing, and un-man-making college.
>
> Looking forward to meeting you or your successor in office in a place and on a day you do not expect.
>
> UnYours Faithlessly,
>
> Musisi

By the time the Principal finished reading the note, and blinked continuously for several seconds before stiffly getting to his feet, Musisi was nowhere to be seen in the college.

Within minutes, the Principal dictated to his secretary a circular to be pinned up on all notice boards in the college spelling out that the Makerere College Political Club was with immediate effect indefinitely dissolved.

All efforts by the Principal in the subsequent weeks to locate and catch Musisi via his old school and his home District office proved utterly fruitless.

* * *

Lwanga and Mwambu read about the dissolution of the Political Club with consternation.

'What the hell!' Lwanga swore at the Library wall on which hang the Principal's circular about the dissolution of the club. 'What the hell, I say!'

Back in the hall, he and Mwambu vented their fury and disgust in volumes of phrases and terms denoting utter distaste.

'You know what?' Mwambu carried on the tirade. 'This Principal reminds me of my former Headmaster and my Physics teacher at Elgon Secondary School. The three are just the same! They're afraid. They're afraid of being challenged by students.'

'It's more than that,' Lwanga cut in. 'They're afraid of students who think. And they're the more afraid if those students are black. And they must be just as afraid if the students are yellowish, as in India and Pakistan, or reddish, as in indigenous America. They're afraid because the students, and all indigenous peoples, aren't their own pink colour!'

'They're also afraid that their skin colour will not always be in command.'

'And that their honeymoon in the colonies will soon be cut short.'

'In the colonies, yes – and specifically in those misnomers, such as Uganda, known as "Protectorates"!'

They wound up their castigation of the British Empire upon noticing that it was getting quite late in the afternoon.

'And now it's time,' Mwambu wistfully observed, 'we proceed to perform one of the so many routine acts in which we slavishly continue to ape His Majesty King George VI, who rules half this hanging world.'

'And what is that one slavish routine act?' Lwanga quizzed.

'Drinking tea at four o'clock prompt!'

*   *   *

Then one day, in Lwanga's final year at the college and Mwambu's penultimate, the biggest news of the decade broke. In a swift overnight move, the Governor of Uganda Protectorate deported His Royal Majesty the Kabaka of Buganda to Britain.

'That can't be true!' exclaimed one astonished man to another on a back street in Kampala.

'Yes, it's true!'

'A mere Governor sending the Lion King of Buganda into exile?'

'So it appears.'

'And to that dwarfish island stupidly called Great Britain, which is no bigger that the size of this Uganda of ours?'

'Yes. But remember that His Royal Majesty Kabaka Mutesa's grandfather, Ssekabaka Mwanga Magulunyondo the Hammer-legged One, Lion of Buganda, was once deported by the same insolent powers to an even tinier island than Britain, the Seychelles, which is a finite dot in the Indian Ocean.'

'How very true that is! How very true, I say! But how long shall we suffer this insult, this urinating upon the heads of royalty by these albino nobodies? How long, I ask you?'

'You ask me another one!'

'Surely, when a youngster or gangster, like this Governor appears to be, behaves crudely before his seniors, we normally ask him, "Are there no elders where you come from?" '

'It seems indeed that there're no elders worthy of respect in that infinitesimal Great Britain of theirs. The people there have no manners, and no good breeding.'

'It must be so. Otherwise how could this Governor, in the very first place, have dared to quarrel with His Royal Majesty the Kabaka?'

'Are you saying that they quarrelled?'

'Yes, that's what everybody is saying. That they disagreed and quarrelled.'

'Disagreed and quarrelled about what, if I may ask?'

'About nothing, they say.'

'About nothing? That's impossible.'

'Well, what do men, two men normally quarrel about?'

'You know the answer very well. They quarrel about land, animal wealth and women.'

'And so which of those three threw them into a quarrel?'

'It was none of them. I've told you it was caused by nothing.'

'But who started the quarrel? Who of them went to the other's house to start the great quarrel about the great nothing?'

'The Kabaka went near the Governor, but he didn't start the quarrel, you can be sure.'

'What! The Lion went to the house of a mere Squirrel? Never! That can't have happened.'

'It's exactly as you say. The truth is that that Governor isn't a Squirrel. He's Wakayima the Hare.'

'That's the very reason why His Majesty shouldn't have gone to or near the home of Hare the trickster!'

'What people are saying is that His Majesty didn't go to Hare's house or home as such. He happened to be on a royal tour of his territories in those parts where Hare's house is located. When Hare saw His Majesty's entourage, he craftily played the part of a humble foreign subject. He invited His Majesty and his entourage to make a brief stopover in the canvas shade outside his house and have some rest with simple refreshments. His Majesty, they say, graciously granted the request. And that's when the dirty, ugly, rude, crude, cunning, wily, insufferable, uncouth and ill-bred trick was played upon His Majesty. Several muscular men in waiters' uniforms walked up to His Majesty with serving trays bearing bottles and glasses – and simply spirited His Majesty away into a waiting Landover belonging to Hare, the Governor. At least that's the version that I've been told.'

'Be that as it may, the incomparable glory of Buganda is from long, long ago! And it will never end! Long live His Royal Majesty Ssabasajja Kabaka!'

IX
Glimpses of Home

Mwambu invariably went back home for all his college vacations. And every vacation he remained a novelty to his village folk. Both the young and old asked him endless questions about Makerere. Did it have one big building or many buildings? Was it bigger or smaller than Elgonton town? Was it true that all the teachers there were pink men from King George's faraway country beyond the deserts and seas? Was the pink man's language spoken at the college spoken through the mouth or through the nose? And why did all pink people speak as if they had no teeth in their mouths? Yes, why did their language always sound like it was coming from a mouth that had no teeth and gums, so that all one could hear was *fwoti-fwoti-fwoti fwe-fwe-fwe*?

To escape the perpetual questions, Mwambu sometimes went on lone walks upon one hill or another. One particular afternoon up on the hill above his home, he relived some scenes of his infant and childhood days.

...Come, Mwambu. I Nerima will be your wife when we grow up. Come let's walk through the fields of yam, up to that tall ash tree in the middle. Let's part the young undergrowth. Let's break some tender branches of the broad-leaved kumufwoora and spread them as our mattress upon the cool soft earth. Now I have spread my loincloth upon the leaves. You too take off your wrapper, and let's for ever lie here together side by side...

...As I am Kangala, I know what you Mwambu, my best friend, have been up to with my little sister!

Playing man and wife at the age of seven! Well, I guess I must commend you for it. What you were playing at proves that you're a man-child, not a rotten egg. Maybe you should have started long ago, with some different little girl, of course, when you were still eating dust...Ha-ha-ha...

...But I must warn you, Mwambu. Do you know Nakimyeti son of Tsema? Have I never told you what happened to him when he was still a very small boy? No, I have never? Well, small as he was then, he was already as crazy as a he-goat for women. So one day he goes and jumps on a big girl, and when he is right in the middle of it all, he abruptly screams like a child with a big sore suddenly pecked by a hen. And when he comes out, he is bleeding real red! His tiny manhood has been un-skinned right back to its base! So his father called a circumciser and he cut off Nakimyeti's torn foreskin for him. As for the girl, she nearly hanged herself when the women of the village composed a song about her and sang it as they ground their millet upon the grinding-stones:

Nafuuna the daughter of BaMakambo,
Nafuuna O how she over-gauged the number,
Nafuuna O how she un-skinned the snake –
And quickly sucked all its poison!

But for Nakimyeti, from that very day he stopped growing! That's how, they say, he became a dwarf. That's how he came to remain half the height of his younger brother!

* * *

And another afternoon, in a dark, fidgety mood, Mwambu rode a bicycle to his sister's home. His five-year-old nephew Masa saw him approaching and skipped to meet him.

'That's Uncle!' chanted Masa. 'That's Uncle! That's Uncle!'

'And that's Nephew! That's Nephew!' Mwambu reciprocated, brightening up.

Little Masa took hold of the left horn of the bicycle while Mwambu kept his grip on the right horn with his right hand stretched above Masa's head and, between the two of them, they steered the machine to the veranda and rested it against the wall. Mwambu was welcomed inside the neat mud-and-wattle grass-thatched house, and a foldable wooden chair was opened out for him. Amid repeated greetings from his sister Khalayi and Murumbi her husband and the twisting of the baby in Khalayi's arms, Masa kept on plying his uncle with curious questions.

'Uncle,' he called as he cosily sat himself on Mwambu's knee and looked up into his eyes in pure delight.

'Yes, nephew of mine,' Mwambu cheerfully replied.

'Does your bicycle have eyes?'

'No, it does not. Not even ears and nose.'

'Then how does it see?'

'But it does not see.'

'So how does it know where it is going? How does it stay on the path and not run into the trees near the path?'

'I tell it where to go.'

'You tell it? But you said it has no ears.'

Mwambu could see he was already in problems with his little nephew the philosopher.

'True, it has no ears. Let's say that I hold it on the path and keep pushing it forward. I do that with my feet as they firmly go up and down working on those bits of metal which stick out from the middle of the bicycle.'

'And you don't fall off?'

'No, I don't fall off. I keep very firm on it, moving my body from side to side slightly, like I'm doing now for you It's called balancing.'

'And it goes anywhere you like?'

'Yes, it goes anywhere – on the path.'

'Shall we go to heaven on it, Uncle?'

'And where is heaven?' Mwambu inquisitively returned, suddenly realising his own childhood seated upon his knee.

'Up there,' Masa confidently replied, pointing towards the roof.

'Ah-ha!' exhaled Mwambu. 'Then we can't go there on a bicycle.'

'Oh, can't we?' Masa was visibly puzzled. 'So how shall we go there?'

'Upon our knees,' was the ready answer.

'Upon our knees!' exclaimed Masa. 'Uncle, you're lying!'

'What's that I hear?' Khalayi sternly cut in as she returned from the kitchen. 'Is it you Masa I hear calling your grown-up uncle a liar?'

Setting a calabash of warm millet brew on a small table before Mwambu, she pulled Masa from his uncle's knee.

'Run along and play outside,' she directed. 'And let your uncle drink something in peace.'

'But mother,' protested Masa, fondly returning to Mwambu's knee and radiating a smile, 'Uncle lied very nicely.'

'Uncle told a lie, you insolent child?' fumed Khalayi.

'Yes, mother, before you came in. He lied that we can walk to heaven on our knees.'

'Oh no,' laughed Mwambu. 'Masa, I didn't say we *walk* on our knees. I said we *go* to heaven on our knees. I said so because it is on our knees that we pray to God best. It is when we are on our knees that God opens the door of heaven to us.'

'Ah!' marvelled Masa, raising his eyes towards the roof.

'But of course,' Mwambu continued, 'you can go to heaven standing up, Masa. Or while you're seated down or even while you're lying on your stomach.'

'And also on your back, Uncle? Masa's imagination was in flight.

'Yes, yes, you can do it on your back.'

Masa's disbelief expressed itself in dilated eyes and a parted mouth. And for a fleeting moment, Mwambu caught a glimpse of himself on his back upon a hospital stretcher on his circumcision day. *Would I have gone to heaven if the anesthetic administered to me had killed me there and then?*

'Uncle,' Masa pressed, 'and go to heaven on your back?'

'Ye- e- e-s, nephew of mine,' stammered Mwambu. 'Yes, you can get to heaven like that.'

Greatly disappointed, he jumped down from Mwambu's knee and made a beeline for the green grass outside. For he would have so much preferred to arrive in heaven *up there* in wonderful style, riding on the back of his uncle's fantastic bicycle, and not sliding upon his stomach or backside.

And Mwambu, as he sipped from the millet brew calabash, wryly savoured Masa's infant words: *Uncle, you said the bicycle has no ears... And go to heaven on your back? Uncle, you're lying...But mother, Uncle lied very nicely...*

*   *   *

Towards the end of most vacations, Mwambu did farewell rounds to the homesteads of his favourite aunts and uncles. Very often he was treated to a savoury meal of plantain and chicken curry. Then after the savoury meal, the uncle and aunt would bid him a lengthy goodbye, interjected with hints of favours that were hopefully expected from him when he became an important government worker with a fat salary.

'May you be tireless in reading books,' the wife of his youngest maternal uncle prayerfully invoked at the end of Mwambu's third visit to the home. 'Then will you one day surely look upon us with a generous eye.'

'Yes, aunt, if it's God's wish,' Mwambu politely replied.

'And then will you also take away the blindness,' she continued, 'from the eyes of these little brothers and sisters of yours; so that they too may see the world with eyes that have been inside a school.'

A naked specimen of the little brothers, on sensing that he was being referred to, retreated behind the mother's wrapper of a soil-brown colour that had once been of an off-white colour.

'For they have nobody but you,' she appealingly concluded, pulling the shy specimen from his temporary hideout behind her and placing him between Mwambu and herself.

In another homestead, the widow of a paternal uncle was so excited to see Mwambu she slew for him a fat hen and prepared for him a special millet meal of freshly harvested finger millet. The aunt specially placed the gizzard – popularly known as 'the major chicken' – in Mwambu's soup bowl to signify as to who the honoured guest of the meal was.

His lean-looking grown-up cousins keenly joined Mwambu at the humble table and helped themselves to the impressive mountain of the millet meal with much relish, causing its disappearance in record time.

As if previously rehearsed, the tummy-full eldest cousin gave a belch of satisfaction upon the conclusion of the self-assigned gastronomic task.

'What the ancients said is really true,' he pleasantly observed, 'that the visitor is the saviour of his host. Because, as you can see, our beloved Mwambu,' he added, wiping perspiration from his forehead with his bare left palm, 'you have caused mother's good chicken to be eaten by us all.'

Mwambu replied with a contrived smile, trying to conceal his amazement at his cousins' mammoth appetites.

'May you come visiting us as many times,' continued the cousin, comically stroking his belly, 'as my mouldy inside cries out for something sweet and special.'

Ignoring the cousin's blabbering, Mwambu offered his compliments to the aunt.

'Thank you very much, mother,' he said, 'for enduring the smoke to prepare this wonderful meal for us.'

'And thank you too,' warmly returned the aunt, 'for eating a little.' She paused for a while, and then went on. 'Food we have, but what should be eaten with it is what we don't have.'

'Oh, we couldn't have eaten better than this, mother,' Mwambu protested.

'Yes, we could have,' she countered. 'There're no real chickens in the land these days. Today we have indeed fed only the lower lip. One day maybe we shall feed the upper lip also. If things were good, when the son of my husband's very brother comes to see me like this, I would fall the largest cock in the compound.'

'Don't say that, mother! The so very good food that I've eaten will be surprised at you and rebel in my inside.'

'All right, all right, let it be as you say,' the aunt conceded. 'I'll stop there.'

The gourmandising cousins had cleared out of the house as soon as their appetites had been served. After a good while, Mwambu rose to his feet meaning to bid farewell to the aunt but she restrained him with her eyes to resume his seat.

'To eat we have eaten, Mwambu my son,' she said, apparently reverting to the subject of food. 'But as you see me your mother, I don't have a drop of paraffin in this house. If I don't cry before you, before whom shall I cry?'

Mwambu quickly absorbed a streak of embarrassment.

'In telling me of this, mother,' he managed to say, 'you're completely right. The old ones say that "The goat that does not cry out" –'

'– "Dies on its tether",' the aunt completed the proverb. 'Yes, my child,' she carried on, 'and they also say that "The beggar is better" –'

'– "Than the thief",' Mwambu added.

'As for me NabuSukuya the daughter of BaSukuya,' she swore, spitting saliva into her right palm and waving it in the air, 'I'd rather die of poverty than steal to become rich. Ask your mother. She has known me ever since she married into this clan.'

Deep in his inside, Mwambu was marvelling at the generous hospitality that will slay a choice hen for a visitor and then turn round and ask the visitor for paraffin worth only one egg. The hospitality and the economics did not rhyme.

As he was leaving, he reached into his right hind pocket and produced a silver coin for the aunt. She thanked him in many different ways for the so, so little. She slightly spat saliva onto both his palms in blessing and raised his hands to the sky.

'I pronounce that you become the vegetable *indelema*,' she intoned, 'that creeps across and survives all dry seasons. I pronounce that you become everlasting like Namisindwa Ridge, the splendour of Masaaba's Mountain. Let those who speak evil about you go downward while you go upward...'

The invocations kept echoing in his head as he walked towards home, while Masaaba's Mountain, bathed in the golden light of the setting sun, majestically held up the eastern horizon.

* * *

Quite early in his youth, Mwambu had promoted himself from his teenage one-room square house of mud walls and a roof thatch of woven dry banana fibres. With savings from his District bursary to the university over the first three years, he had constructed himself a rectangular two-bedroom house with walls of sun-dried bricks and a roof of galvanised iron sheets. It had a cemented floor and plastered walls. Located on the upper side of the slope, one stone throw away from his father's grass-thatched mud-and-wattle round house, it became one of the spectacular houses numbering not more than the fingers on both hands that boasted of a galvanised iron roof for as far as the eye could see in all directions. And because Mwambu had had its outside walls painted the light blue colour of the sky, the villagers humorously nick-named it 'The Sky House', thereby meaning that its occupier was somebody whose feet may be set upon the firm soil but whose head was in the clouds.

During the long vacation at the end of his fourth year at the university, Mwambu was one early morning washing his face outside his house when his cousin Kuloba came walking briskly along the footpath that ran between Mwambu's house and his father's. He seemed to be going on an urgent journey but on seeing Mwambu, he abruptly stopped.

'Hey, son of the clan,' he called out, 'greetings of peace to you.'

'Greetings of peace to you too, elder,' Mwambu replied, straightening up and placing his mug of water on a nearby flat stone.

Kuloba considered Mwambu intensely in a moment of silence, and then burst out bluntly.

'Mwambu, what has happened to you, such that you no longer visit some of us your relatives?'

'Oh, um, um," stammered Mwambu. 'I do try to visit around as much as I can.'

'Yes, yes,' Kuloba countered, 'but you're too proud, or too something else to come down to some of our miserable homes.' His tone conveyed both sarcasm and censure.

'Don't say that, elder,' Mwambu firmly replied. 'You know very well that failure to visit and check on kinsfolk is often not a matter of one's being proud but a result of laziness, that repeatedly puts off an intended visit.'

'I don't agree with you there,' Kuloba countered. 'Otherwise how was it,' he continued with a sardonic smile, 'that when you were in secondary school, you found your way to my house everyday of every vacation? Or was it because', he hit home, 'in those years I was away with the King's African Rifles fighting in the Second World War, and you were much happier visiting Mayuba my wife in her loneliness?'

'Kuloba my elder!' Mwambu called out from somewhere deep inside him. 'What are you accusing me of?'

'Accusing you, am I? No, I'm not. I'm accusing you of nothing.'

O God, he bears me a deathless grudge! 'Well then,' Mwambu sarcastically breathed, 'thank you for accusing me of nothing.'

'That's right,' Kuloba ambiguously reciprocated, 'because if there was anything I should accuse you of, you would have yourself known what it is.'

And so saying, Kuloba turned round to walk back towards his home, leaving Mwambu with a crestfallen face, his right forefinger upon his mouth. He was wondering if Kuloba had been proceeding on a genuine journey which he had now suddenly cancelled, or whether he had purposely come all the way to pretend that Mwambu owed him a visit while actually insinuating that he owed him something else. *Mwambu, what has happened to*

*you? ...but you're too proud or too something else...much
happier visiting Mayuba my wife in her loneliness...I'm
accusing you of...of nothing...you would have yourself
known what it is...*

*   *   *

The following day, in the cool of early evening, Mwambu
was reading a book in the shade of a mango tree close by his
bachelor house, while the faraway everlasting mountain
displayed its majestic splendour under a cloudless sky.
Casually looking up at some random moment, he was
pleasantly surprised to see his childhood friend Kangala
walking towards him.

'Child of the Ancients,' he called out, excitedly getting
to his feet, 'I'm very happy to see you!'

'Same with me, Child of the Ancients,' Kangala
reciprocated as they noisily struck hands in a hearty
greeting.

Child of the Ancients is what they had fondly called
each other ever since the days of their early boyhood,
taken from the words of a circumcision song very popular
at the time.

Mwana we Bataayi syalelo –	Child of the Ancients today –
Bakeni bamakana bakharure!	Visitors fantastic will appear!

'Sit down, sit down, my Visitor Fantastic,' Mwambu
enthused, pointing Kangala to the spare folding wooden
chair. 'It's been many seasons since I last set eyes on you.
And that's surely understandable, after you acquired more
land across the valley and planted your second wife there.'

'I don't know about planting wives,' Kangala cheerfully
replied. 'What I know is that I'm now the owner of land
upon two neighbouring hillsides, and that my name is fast
sinking its roots on both sides of River Nabarwa, the river
of mankind's genesis.

'Ah, that sounds so antique and true,' Mwambu complimented. 'But tell me,' he jovially continued, 'how does it feel like to be husband of two wives?'

'I'll sure tell you if you'll first tell me,' Kuloba naughtily countered, 'what it feels like at your ripe age to be husband of not even one.'

Mwambu managed a plain smile while he figured out what to say, knowing that marriage was supposed to happen as soon as a boy became a man via the man-maker's circumcision knife.

'You see, Mwambu,' Kangala carried on, 'by now there should have been a woman in this modern and pretty house of yours to warm your bed whenever you come home on vacation. And you would be steadily replacing some of your ancestors who continue un-named in their invisible Magombeland. Or do you already have a wife at that big school of Makerere?'

'No, no,' Mwambu readily answered with a warm smile. 'But let me assure you that one of these days I'll bring somebody's daughter home, and you will be among the first few to know about it – about her.'

'Let me hope so, Child of the Ancients. 'And let me hope that she'll be a fertile one, not one with ash in her womb, like the wife of that Reverend Matamali who baptised you many, many seasons ago.'

'What you mean,' Mwambu musingly replied, 'is that Reverend Matamali's wife has never had a child.' And the words of his favourite but difficult verse from Prophet Isaiah corkscrewed through his head – *Rejoice, O barren one, who never bore a child; burst into song, and shout for joy, you who were never in labour, for more are the children of the desolate woman than of her that has a husband...*

'Not only that. Neither has her husband ever had a child.'

'Naturally! If your wife doesn't give you a child, then you have no child.'

'Not exactly, as Matamali very well knows, and as everyone around here knows. He tried so hard to have an heir with some extra woman after another. And that's how his well-guarded bedroom secret eventually leaked out.'

'And what was that secret?' Mwambu was getting really curious.

'The secret that one of Matamali's extra women spilt during a millet brew drinking spree one harvest season ago was that the good Reverend had never been circumcised.'

'What!' Mwambu incredulously exclaimed.

'Yes,' Kangala calmly carried on. 'He had been pretending for all that time that he had been cleaned into a man by the knife while still a boy and working as a farm labourer at Kitale in Kenya on a pink man's shamba. That was before he returned to begin going to school when he was old enough to impregnate a woman.'

'The pity of it, I say!' Mwambu stood up as if just to stretch his legs, but much more to disguise the emotional perturbation aroused by all that talk about his highly esteemed baptiser.

'Ah, but the greater pity and scandal is,' Kangala pressed on with his story, 'that at the beginning of the last dry season, after you returned to Kampala at the end of your vacation, as I learnt from your mother, Matamali had to run very fast to the hospital to escape being circumcised by force inside the church –'

'No more, Kangala! No more of that story!' Mwambu was beside himself with anger.

'But what's your problem, Mwambu?' Kangala asked, apparently puzzled, as he also got to his feet. 'Can't you enjoy a pure story like this one?'

'You call that a *pure* story? No, I can't enjoy it!'

'Oh, well, I can see you're actually upset. I'm sorry if I've said something foolish, my friend Mwambu, Child of the Ancients!'

'No, no, you have not,' replied Mwambu, trying to regain his composure.

'Yes, I have not. And I'm certainly not likening *you* to that Matamali. Because I know that in your case, no one chased you around. You voluntarily went to hospital for –'

'Let's talk about something else please!' Mwambu's irritation was approaching breaking point. He walked back to his chair, slumped onto it, and indicated the other chair for Kangala.

'No, no,' Kangala impatiently said, waving both hands. 'I don't have to sit down again. I only came to visit you briefly, and I appear to have done more than that. I better return to my place, across the valley. Stay well, Mwambu.'

'Go well, Kangala,' replied Mwambu without getting up as his friend, Child of the Ancients, walked away.

X

The Creator of Creation Place

Back at college for the next term, Mwambu lay awake on his bed one night, his mind going around his first trip to Kampala. He remembered that early in his first year he had mentioned the subject of Katonda we Butonda to Lwanga, as introduced to him by the enigmatic elderly man called Muntu, and how Muntu had abruptly disembarked from the bus, telling Mwambu where to find him if he ever desired to see him again. And now Lwanga was in his final year, and he might soon not be readily available as his possible companion to Katonda we Butonda shrine, the notion of which had never left his fancy. He decided to put his request to Lwanga when the latter returned from the library the following afternoon. On being asked, Lwanga gladly promised to accompany him, saying it would be a learning excursion for him as well, or a revision lesson in culture.

* * *

The long anticipated trip finally took place on the last Sunday of Lwanga's penultimate term at the College. The two adventurers got onto the early morning Kampala-Jinja bus. The twelve-mile stretch to Mukono town took them almost an hour as the bus endlessly stopped to pick new passengers on the way. The two hopped off the bus, crossed the road, and jumped onto the back of a pick-up truck headed for the fishing and landing site of Katosi on the shores of Lake Victoria. Six miles later along the dusty murram road, at a place called Namakwa, they alighted from the bone-shaking pick-up truck.

The mid morning sun was radiantly smiling down on one of the most delectable landscapes of Africa, of rival beauty with the enchanting mountains of Ethiopia and the wondrous valleys of the Limpopo River. Mwambu looked all around him to try and fix his bearings. He and Lwanga were standing upon a random spot of idyllic Kyaggwe County. To the sunrise end was Mabira Forest, in that countryside of evergreen broad trees and lush tall grass that had earlier in the century enthralled the British traveller Winston Churchill into baptising it as 'The Pearl of Africa'.

Mwambu and Lwanga approached some three men at a nearby house to ask for directions to their destination. After a formal exchange of greetings, Lwanga asked the three how to get to the shrine at Butonda.

'You have your backs right against it,' said Lusangwa, the youngest of the three.

'Is that so?' Lwanga replied. 'And how far is it?'

'D'you see that tall Mvule tree at the top of this gentle rise? From there to the shrine is the same distance as from the same tree to where we are.'

'That's quite a long walk, isn't it?'

'Yes, it will take you as long as it takes our women to walk to the well and back.'

'Which means that your well is not very near,' Lwanga remarked, trying to establish as much rapport with the three men as possible.

'That's true,' replied Lusangwa. 'But instead of going by yourselves,' Lusangwa venture to say in his own interest, 'why don't you ask me to accompany you as your guide and protector?'

'As protector? Against what?' Lwanga keenly queried him.

'Oh, you never know,' Lusangwa promptly replied with a shrug of the shoulders. 'It could be against snakes or lions, for example – and I happen to understand their ways and hunting times very well.'

After a bit of good-hearted haggling, a deal was struck to the effect that Lusangwa was to act as guide for a cash equivalent of a small bottle of waragi, Uganda's 'war gin' ever since World War II.

When the trio got to the shrine, Mwambu was at once struck by the obvious ordinariness of the shrine and its immediate environs. He was amazed that the divine could be no more impressive than what he was seeing. Before them, constituting the entire shrine and surrounded by short but uncut grass, was a simple edifice of grass-thatched mud-and-wattle round hut with a small wooden door that was half open at the time.

A few paces away under a huge mango tree were seated a handful of male and female supplicants in various postures and sundry plain attires. Some had come to inquire about their worrying personal situations from *balubaale,* the spirits of eminent ancestors; others had come to celebrate their victories and successes with basketfuls of food to be eaten in the presence of the respective gods in charge of individual aspects of human endeavour: marriage, procreation, good health, plentiful harvest, and a host of others.

One of the worshippers in particular had just told fellow supplicants that he had come to intercede with the gods whose anger had put his younger brother under a terrible curse. The younger brother, the supplicant narrated, had infuriated the gods by uttering blasphemy and neglecting to offer any sacrifice for many seasons; and consequently, the angry gods had decreed a severe curse on him. Three days earlier the young man's tongue had suddenly started growing out of his mouth. It grew and grew, and all that his family could do to help him was to coil the elongated tongue into several folds in a large raffia basket.

'What's the name of the chief custodian of the shrine?' Mwambu asked Lusangwa.

'He's called Muntu.'

Mwambu nodded with satisfaction at the thought of his meeting Muntu again. 'So is he right now at the shrine or not?'

'When the door is half open, as it is now, it means that he is not around.'

'And if it's wide open, or shut?'

'If it's wide open, he's around. If it's closed, then neither he nor his assistant custodian is around.'

'Ah, that's really interesting. So where is the assistant custodian?'

'The meaning of the door being half open is that the assistant custodian is in there.'

'I see,' marvelled Mwambu. 'Is it possible for us to enter the shrine?'

Lusangwa peeped into the shrine, and noticed that Musisi, the assistant shrine custodian, was performing his daily rituals of symbolic gestures accompanied by soft declamatory utterances.

Taking off his plastic sandals, Lusangwa stepped inside the hut and beseeched Musisi to receive what he described as two young supplicants from the city.

'Let them in,' intoned Musisi from the semi-darkness behind the partition of a straw mat.

In, stepped Lwanga and Mwambu; Mwambu immediately took in the ceremonial regalia of the shrine keeper's profession: a large drum in the centre, a shield leaning against the wall, a buffalo horn and several strings of cowries hanging on the wall, and five spears planted in the ground to the right; and to the left a hoe, a machete, a club, five calabashes containing divination stones, and a fireplace marked by three ashy hearth-stones.

'Who are you?' demanded Musisi in a guttural voice, remaining behind the partition so that his face could not be made out. 'And where have you come from?'

'I'm Lwanga.'

'And I'm called Mwambu.'

'What's your totem, Lwanga?'

'I'm of the Lungfish clan.'

'And you Mwambu, what's yours?'

'My totem,' Mwambu shakily improvised on the spot, 'is the Circumcision Knife.'

'Liar!' Musisi angrily charged. 'A knife is not one of BuGanda's fifty-two totems. What's your clan, you liar?'

'Mine is not one of your fifty-two,' Mwambu replied as courageously as he could; 'it is the ancestor of all your fifty-two and – '

'What!'

'Yes, sir, mine is not a clan but an entire people – BaMasaaba of Masaabaland.'

'Then you're in the wrong place! You stranger, how dare you come to the shrine of the Creator of creation? How dare you come from beyond to the Creator's Creation Place?'

'Because if he is the Creator of all creation,' Mwambu fearlessly countered, 'then he must be Creator of Masaabaland and me. And that's why I have come to worship him at the spot from where he reaches out to everything in existence. Do you dare begrudge me by calling me a stranger? Or did a minor god create BuGanda, while the rest of the world was created by a major god that we do not know?'

'Off with your *lugezigezi*, your bookish cleverness! But tell me,' said Musisi, somewhat relenting, 'what exactly did you come to do here?'

'To tell you the whole truth: I came to visit my friend Muntu, your boss.'

'You're mad, young man!' Musisi fumed. 'How can Muntu, the chief custodian of this holy shrine, be a friend of a nonentity like you? And don't call Muntu my boss, because he's not. He's only a human being; but whereas I stoop to act as his assistant, I am actually the god of –'

'What!' exclaimed Mwambu and Lwanga in astounded unison.

'To prove which, as an all-knowing god, let me tell you your full names and your occupations. You're Charles Lwanga; and you're Abraham Mwambu.'

Lwanga and Mwambu were utterly astonished.

'You Lwanga,' Musisi assuredly continued, 'are a final year student at Makerere's so-called Department of Education; and you Mwambu are a second year Arts student at the same Makerere's Department of Ignorance.'

'Institute of what?' Lwanga incredulously asked, as he and Mwambu blinked at each other, hearing their apex of learning thus derogatively described.

'And the two of you,' Musisi pressed on, 'were respectively President and Committee Member of the last Executive of Makerere College Political Club which was indefinitely suspended for – '

'I have a brain wave!' Mwambu rapturously called out.

'Which was indefinitely suspended for having had an outgoing President who –'

'I have a brainwave! ' Mwambu announced again, entranced.

'Who was a god disguised as a student of –'

'My brainwave! ' Mwambu exploded the words. 'My brainwave tells me, that you Mr. Assistant Custodian of the shrine of Katonda we Butonda – are M^2, Michael Musisi! You're that previous President of Makerere College Political Club!'

Lwanga: 'Impossible!'

Mwambu: 'Unthinkable and true!'

Musisi: 'Yes, my successors in office – I am Michael Musisi.'

* * *

On their way out from the shrine, Mwambu and Lwanga met Muntu on his way in to report for duty. They introduced themselves to him, and Mwambu reminded him of their first meeting on the Elgonton-Kampala bus.

'Ah, that's years ago,' remarked Muntu amiably.

'Yes. And because you left me an open invitation to come and visit you, that's why I've made it today, in the company of my friend here.'

'But that was on a certain condition,' Muntu reminded Mwambu.

'Which I do still remember; it was that if I ever needed your company again on life's journey.'

'That's right. And did you,' Muntu pressed on, 'eventually need that company today?'

'Yes, there was this undying urge in me to come and see you in your professional habitat. But I didn't know what profession it really was until we got here. So you're an intercessor between men and the gods!'

'Yes, you can call me that,' Muntu conceded.

'And your assistant is called Musisi.'

'Not at all,' Muntu firmly asserted.

'What do you mean by that?' Mwambu was genuinely puzzled.

'All custodians and assistant custodians of the shrine of Katonda we Butonda,' Muntu explained, 'must automatically come from the Elephant clan. And anyone by the name Musisi obviously belongs to the Dog clan, and therefore cannot be a shrine custodian! In other words, anyone with the name of a god (lubaale) is too divine to be a shrine custodian. The name of my assistant custodian, who you've just seen, is actually Mbazzi of the Elephant clan – not Musisi.

For the second time that morning Mwambu and Lwanga blinked at each other with incredulous faces.

'Ah, but maybe,' Mwambu suggested, scratching his head for an idea, 'Mbazzi is also Musisi. And since Musisi bears the name of a god, maybe he can divinely condescend to perform a role that befits Mbazzi or –'

'No, he can't!' Muntu exclaimed.

'Well, well, old one,' Lwanga butted in, more confused than comprehending, 'perhaps you can sort that out with Musisi-Mbazzi while we take our leave.'

'Oh yes, you had better do that. Go well, young men.'

'Stay well, elder,' said Lwanga.

'Stay well, elder,' Mwambu added.

XI
Forth with Torches of Knowledge

How time passes! So Mwambu wondered. For the one academic year plus one term that succeeded the visit to Butonda shrine had flown unusually fast. Before he knew what, his friend Lwanga graduated and went to start out on his teaching career in a suburban high school. And this particular afternoon words about time flux from two favourite hymns of Mwambu's secondary school days came rhythmically flashing onto his interior screen:

A thousand ages in thy sight
Are like an evening gone...

Yet nearer and nearer draws the time
The time that shall surely be –
When the earth shall be filled with the glory of God
As the waters cover the sea...

His mind skipped back to an afternoon during Lwanga's final term at the college, when as he lay on his back upon the bed, his thoughts lingered around Lwanga reading for his approaching final exams. He recalled musing generally on students' self appellation as 'seekers of the truth'. When they wanted to vary this perception of themselves, they called themselves 'pursuers of the flame of knowledge'. The duration of their pursuit of that flame varied a great deal. Some chose to call off the pursuit upon the proverbial hill after the two certificate years. Others opted to continue to one or the other of the two-year further, diploma pursuits.

Yet others went on to three-year further pursuits leading to degree awards of a general or professional nature.

Having opted for Education and Humanities, respectively, Lwanga and Mwambu progressively discovered what many before them had discovered – that the more sparks of the flame of knowledge they acquired, the less knowledgeable they became!

'I think that acquiring more and more knowledge,' remarked Lwanga, returning from the library in a reflective mood and seating himself on Mwambu's bed, 'is like climbing a tree. The higher you climb, the further away you get from the roots and stem of the tree.'

'I agree with that,' replied Mwambu. 'Isn't that what's called knowing more and more about less and less?'

'Correct. Let's say that in primary school you climb up the stem of the tree. In secondary school you climb onto a branch. At college you climb onto a branch-let.'

'With a first degree,' Mwambu continued in Lwanga's vein, 'you climb onto a branch-ling. With a Masters degree you climb onto a leaf. And –'

'And with a doctorate,' Lwanga quickly cut in, 'you fall off the tree!'

They laughed merrily together at their own intellectual buffoonery. After which Lwanga felt his low spirits rising again and he rose up to proceed to his room.

* * *

And now – another year gone by – it was Mwambu's turn to graduate. As he sat in the exalted graduation hall, he recalled the registration day on his first arrival at the college and Mr. Robinson, the Registrar, ambiguously telling him that he was a student with a blank in his character, on account of having a blank testimonial from his former headmaster – and that he, the Registrar, would keep an eye on him. *It's upon you to decide what happens to that blank during your stay on this campus,* he remembered Mr. Robinson saying. But not once did Mwambu have the uncanny feeling of being spied upon by some big hidden eye. Had Mr. Robinson forgotten about him immediately, or had he perhaps –

'By virtue of the authority bestowed upon me,' the Chancellor's voice reverberated around the exalted hall, 'I constitute this assembly into the Ninth Congregation of Makerere University College, University of London.'

The solemn announcement was followed by the routine presentation of graduands to the Chancellor by their respective Deans. Since the total number of the graduating students was just slightly over fifty, the Chancellor took off his academic hat and successively rested it on the head of each one. One by one they knelt before him: the chancellor called the particular initiate by name as he pronounced the magic words of conferment of the degree award.

'By virtue of the authority entrusted to me, I confer upon you – James Byaruhanga – the degree of Bachelor of Education.'

Applause and ululations.

'By virtue of the authority entrusted to me, I confer upon you – Wilson Matovu – the degree of Bachelor of Science.'

Applause and prolonged ululations.

'By virtue of the authority entrusted to me, I confer upon you – Abraham Mwambu – the degree of Bachelor of Arts.'

Applause and highest ululations.

Back on his feet to return to his seat, Mwambu was all bubbles of ultimate sensation. He felt like he was walking on air, floating on clouds of achievement. *Clap; clap your hands, invisible dwellers of land and sky! Clap; clap your*

111

hands, all things bright and beautiful, all creatures of rivers and seas! For today, I Mwambu have climbed the tree of knowledge – as far as the terminal branches...

He was chimed back from fantasyland by the concluding remarks in the Chancellor's speech.

'To you graduates of this singular day, I say the following. This is your day of commissioning, your day of passage from your past phase of life to the next. It is your day of transiting from being intellectual youngsters to intellectual adults. It is your day of transitioning from students to workers in the marketplace – of maturing from being economic beneficiaries to being economic benefactors.

'You have been equipped with the intellectual and professional tools necessary for guaranteeing your personal and your family's wellbeing, as well as causing positive change in your immediate communities and the wider society - of your entire country. We have provided you with dynamic packages of knowledge and professional kits that include stethoscopes and blackboard chalk! As a foundation to all your academic attainments, we have provided you with general practical knowledge and a capacity for appreciation: such that each one of you, regardless of your particular intellectual discipline – should be able to mend a broken fuse in an electric circuit, cultivate flowers as a mark of your love of beauty, and show compassion whenever you come across pain in others!

'Or let me say that we have placed in the hands of each one of you a mystery torch. Go forth bearing this mystery torch. Blaze a trail as you go and wherever you go. With this torch of the mind and the spirit, go and cause a revolution wherever you find yourselves – and push back the boundaries of darkness.

'I'm most gratified in believing that we're passing out intellectually full-grown men and women. And I'm depending on you all not to let me down by betraying the confidence I have placed in you...'

And I'm depending on you all not to let me down by betraying the confidence I have in you... Mwambu hypnotically repeated the Chancellor's words from somewhere deep-most in his inside. *Be able to mend a fuse, cultivate flowers, and show compassion...dynamic packages of knowledge and professional kits ...with the mystery torch of the mind...push back the boundaries of darkness ...*

'And now, by virtue of the authority entrusted to me,' the Chancellor's voice rang out in concluding tones that pushed Mwambu to sit up afresh, 'it is my pleasant and bounden duty to declare this Ninth Congregation of Makerere University College, University of London, closed.'

XII

A Whirlwind of Change

Nakintu had completed Nurses' Training College two years ahead of Mwambu's graduation and she was already in employment as a Nursing Officer with the Protectorate Government. By now going steady in their friendship, she and Mwambu exchanged occasional visits and fondly looked forward to a future together. But Mwambu promised himself to first find a job before turning his thoughts to matters of the heart.

And into the marketplace he went immediately upon graduation. And it so happened that his first work station was in the office of the Clerk to the Legislative Council (LEGCO) of Uganda, as an Assistant Clerk to the expatriate boss posted from London. Being a Protectorate of the British Crown, the country was directly governed from London through edicts issued by The Queen in the House of Commons and administered by the Protectorate Governor.

In the discharge of his daily duties, Mwambu thus came into direct contact with the colonial machinery. It was machinery, he angrily told himself, designed to perpetuate the British Empire world without end, stretching as it did across the entire globe, such that its exploiters could sit back at headquarters and thump their chests about the incomparable empire on which the sun never set. And it pained him to the very core that for centuries the exploiters had monstrously plundered the wealth of their so-called overseas dominions, territories, colonies and other possessions: slaves, precious metals, spices, tropical cereals, fruits, sugar, rubber, and a host of raw materials – in exchange for trinkets, mirrors and plastic toys for the dispossessed indigenous peoples.

115

Then the year 1957 suddenly whipped up a whirlwind of change over Africa!

'The British Empire was destined to crack up,' Kwame Nkrumah of the Gold Coast was quoted as saying from a campaign platform in Accra, to the enchantment of political activists dotted all over the African continent.

'The British Empire indeed started cracking up long ago,' he declared. 'Mahatma Gandhi shot the initial volley at the British imperial statue of gold and bronze – and feet of clay. 'Like Nebuchadnezzar and Belshazzar's Babylonian empire of old, the British Empire is about to come to an abrupt end in the middle of the night!

'Ghana oyee!' resounded Nkrumah's charged voice over the football stadium and upon radio airwaves across the continent.

'Osagyefo oyee!' the enchanted continent yelled back.

'Africa oyee!'

'Osagyefo oyee!'

'Africa oyee!'

*　　*　　*

'Did you catch those magic words said by Nkrumah?' Mwambu asked Lwanga with an animated face.

'Which magic words?'

'They were words that he probably made up on the spot, or perhaps words from some ancient or modern inventor of words and song. "O Africa," he said,

> So much to do,
> So little done –
> Such things to be!

Did you catch them – did you catch them, Lwanga? There is magic in words; and there is magic in politics!'

'And worse than magic,' Lwanga replied with a grin.

'In politics, that is. There is hell and bloody thuggery in politics.'

They were now intently listening to the radio relaying the midnight events culminating into Ghana's political independence.

'Do you know what, Mwambu?' Lwanga enthused.

'No, I don't know what,' Mwambu keenly replied.

'This historic day for Ghana – for the Gold Coast that was – is the first African three-cord whip woven from the hide of a hippo that is to break the back of the British camel.'

'Hear, hear!' Mwambu chanted.

'And do you know the final straw that is to finish off this British camel?'

'Yes, I think I do,' replied Mwambu, rising to the challenge of imagination. 'It will be some insignificant coral reef in the Pacific Ocean inhabited by one hundred colonised natives.'

That's right!' Lwanga nodded. 'Or it will be some one-acre colony of unpopulated rock in the West Indies.'

'As for Ghana,' Mwambu continued, reverting to Africa's pace-setter, 'shall I tell you a geo-political mystery?'

'Yes, Mr. Mystical or Mr. Mysterious,' Lwanga joked.

'You know how the British swagger about their tiny, insular superiority – about their being the splendid centre of the world and the terror of the nations.'

'Yes, yes,' replied Lwanga cynically. 'I've been drilled into reading British writers long enough to know that.

This royal throne of kings, this scepter'd isle,
This earth of majesty, this seat of Mars,
This other Eden, demi-paradise,
This fortress built by Nature for herself...
Against the envy of less happier lands
This blessed plot, this earth, this realm, this England...
That England, that was wont to conquer others...
Hath made a shameful conquest of itself...

'Thus pronounces John of Gaunt on his deathbed. And that's your Shakespearian stuff of British nostalgia and patriotism and nationalism and other arrogant sentiments such as self-advancement, self-love, self-interest, self-promotion, self-importance, self-commendation, self-advertisement, self-aggrandisement, and self-exaggeration. But the dying man very precisely foretold the inevitable demise of the unconquerable isles!'

'As conclusively unconquerable,' Mwambu cut in with quick sarcasm, 'as was "absolutely unsinkable" their Titanic that sank on its maiden voyage!'

'Yes, yes! But back to your geo-political mystery – what's mystical about the British telling themselves that they are the tiny centre of the world?'

'You see – to convince, or rather deceive themselves that they are the centre of the globe, they manoeuvre the zero meridian or longitude, which is the so-called prime meridian, to go through London!'

'That they sure do,' Lwanga agreed with a sardonic nod. 'And they make it go through their British Observatory at that!'

'That's right,' Mwambu concurred. 'But what they do not anticipate is that this high-sounding Greenwich meridian of theirs will also run through the main city of the Gold Coast, Accra.'

'That's coincidentally true,' observed Lwanga. 'But where is the mystery?'

'I will tell you. Do you know that the one country in the whole world that is the size of that vaunting little Great Britain of theirs is what has tonight become Ghana?'

'I guess I didn't know that,' Lwanga admitted.

'Don't you see then that the one African country to pioneer the demolition of the British Empire is that which shares Britain's size, and whose capital city shares London's Zero Meridian?'

'Yes, I do see the geographical coincidence,' Lwanga admitted.

'Ah, that which you call coincidence,' Mwambu declaimed with a priestly aura, 'is exactly what I declare to be a geo-political mystery!'

'Mystery, mystics, politics,' Lwanga replied with a broad grin, 'what follows?'

'What follows,' intoned Mwambu, 'is that the African country nearest to Ghana and Britain in size – shall be the first country in the original British East Africa (minus Germany's former territory of Tanganyika) to fire the first regional volley at the already disintegrating British imperial statue with feet of clay.'

'And that country is?' Lwanga quizzed, an incredulous smile playing around his mouth.

'Uganda, of course!'

'Uganda?' Lwanga asked with dilated eyes.

'Yes, Uganda,' Mwambu confidently affirmed.

'That one,' pessimistically announced Lwanga, 'only time will tell.'

'Oh yes,' concurred Mwambu with half-closed, divining eyes, 'only time will tell – and very soon.'

'Uganda oyee!' shouted Lwanga in a mixture of mirth and disbelief.

'Uganda oyee!'

'Africa oyee!'

'Uganda oyee...'

XIII
We Have Come to Pick a Hoe

A few weeks into Ghana's independence, Mwambu decided it was high time he got married. His relationship with Nakintu had grown into permanent courtship. As they had now settled into steady employment, he formally proposed to her the next time she came to visit him at his flat; in the evening, they went out to dance and drink to the occasion.

To acquire a wife, Mwambu remembered an elder telling him in his boyhood days back in the formative village, can be done in one of three ways. When you have spotted the girl you want to marry, you can kidnap her, elope with her, or beg her parents for her. He had been warned against kidnap and elopement as being crude and unmanly, leaving parental consent as the best option.

In pursuit of the this superlative option, and on the advice of Nakintu, Mwambu wrote to Nakintu's parents describing himself as a friend of their daughter and requesting to be allowed to pay them a visit, if possible within the next two moons. In reply, the Reverend Simon Kintu wrote to Mwambu a letter cautiously couched in a neutral tone and named the last Sunday of the following moon as the day for the proposed visit. Consequently, Nakintu travelled back to her parents' home several days before Mwambu's visit, so as to be met there by Mwambu as the truly unknown bride-to-be. She would have to be discovered afresh there, and spotted by Mwambu among a host of daughters of the clan, as the one who especially caught his eye.

When the visiting day arrived, Mwambu's entourage of four saloon cars and a pick-up truck bringing up the rear drove in spectacular style into the large compound of the Kintus. Upon a cue, all the doors of the cars and the pick-up truck simultaneously opened. Out stepped the similar-minded passengers on a mission: the men in navy blue suits, white *kanzus* and black shoes, and each carrying a walking-stick; the women draped in *busuuti* (flowing floral dresses), each of them terminating in glossy dark-brown low heeled shoes.

In a rehearsed fashion, an elder jumped to his feet from among the hosts seated in two concentric semi-circles on low folding wooden chairs in the shade of a tree in front of the main house.

'Who are you,' he sternly demanded, 'and where are you going?'

'We are sojourners from a distant land,' promptly replied the spokesman of Mwambu's entourage, 'now at our journey's terminus.'

'And why are you carrying clubs like warriors headed for a battlefield?'

'These are not clubs, sir, but walking-sticks of weary way-farers,' countered the spokesman. 'Sometimes they do indeed double as hunting-sticks. But we come in peace, not for war.'

'Well, then, hand in your clubs, sticks, or whatever you call them. Hand them in, one by one, all of you.'

'Here they are, sir. We freely yield them to you, one by one.'

'Good. Good sojourners you seem to be. You may now sit down, you and your women, on those spare chairs,' he directed, pointing to chairs arranged in a semi-circle directly facing the hosts.

And so saying, the elder also sat down.

'Thank you, sir. We applaud your kindness to the strangers that we evidently are.'

'But tell me truly,' the elder carried on. 'What manner of men are you, and what manner of women are these women of yours? Where is the land that you inhabit, and what is the object of your sojourn?'

'We are men like all other men; and our women are women like all other women. We come from a land at the front end of the world, where the sun originates from behind a lofty mountain to come and set here over these extensive plains. By profession, we are cultivators of the soil and keepers of cattle across numberless valleys. And it happens that one young man in this company possesses a handle without a hoe, so we have come looking for one such hoe for him in this worthy homestead.'

'You must be a people of metaphors and riddles!' observed the elder, wearing a benign smile. 'Can you change your metaphor?'

'Gladly, sir,' warmly replied the spokesman. 'The purpose of our visit is that one of us may be born in your family.'

'What!' exclaimed the elder in acted surprise.

'And that one of your daughters,' the spokesman pressed on, 'may go and be born in our family.'

The elder and all the hosts marvelled in unison at this apparently amazing proposition, whereupon the elder decided to probe the spokesman further.

'And you, talkative voice of all the rest, who are you? What's your name, and what's your lineage?'

'My name is Kitutu Twaya, son of Wasolo of BaNandutu clan, and grandson of Masolo the valiant one who lies buried with his ancestors on the top of Busoolo hill, that overlooks Masaaba's Mountain.'

'And the presumptuous young man who you say wants to be born in this family – what's his name, and what's his lineage?'

'His name is Mwambu Kiboole, son of Masaaba of BaNamwombe clan, and grandson of Weswa the master warrior who lies buried with his warrior ancestors in the valley of Khantsala.'

In turn, the spokesman of Mwambu's party humbly begged the elder to tell his visitors who he was.

'The name of the one whose voice you're hearing is Walugembe, son of Juuko of the totem-less royal clan. I'm grandson of Kimera who lies in the burial grounds of his exalted forefathers at Gombe.'

'And may we have the honour, sir, and the privilege of being told who the father and the mother of this homestead are, and where they are?'

'For sure, for sure,' obliged the elder, getting back onto his feet, 'you may be told who and where they are. The father of the homestead is the Reverend Simon Kintu; and the mother of the homestead is his dear wife Mukyala Mary. The Reverend Kintu is son of Kakungulu, of the same totem-less royal clan as this speaker. He is grandson to Mwanga who lies in the burial grounds of the forefathers at Kisozi. The Reverend and his wife,' he added, pointing at the couple, 'are those two seated in a sofa right opposite me and –'

A sudden roll of drums of acknowledgement from musicians under a nearby tree and joyous ululations from the women of the clan pleasantly interrupted the elder.

Remaining on his feet, the elder carried on with a brief speech in which he grandly pretended on behalf of the hosts that the abrupt arrival of the visitors had rudely interrupted a clan meeting. And he asked the visitors as to how insolent they could be to go on holding their hosts hostage of the strangers' bad manners, and engaging them in a lengthy dialogue with not a drop of a drink to lubricate their thirsty throats. He wondered if sojourners such as they claimed to be do not carry even unfermented female brew on their journey.

Upon this hint, while the elder took his seat once more, the spokesman deftly signalled to the young men in his party who had been tipped to carry in the huge gourds of banana juice, crates of soft drinks and beers from the back of the pick-up truck. The assorted drinks were immediately brought in and placed in front of the elder to the spontaneous general expression of approving noises by the hosts. The drinks were instantly served around to the hosts, while counterpart banana juice from the host home was generously served around to the visitors.

After the throat lubricants had accomplished their job on both host and guest, the spokesman got onto his feet and requested the elder to permit him to say just one more thing. The permission was happily given.

'Father and mother of this hospitable home, elders and mothers of the clan, and all other members of this enviable clan, if I may be so daring as to presume upon the goodness that you have so far shown to us – we of my party would be more than overjoyed at this point to be shown the subject and destination of our long journey from the mountain to the plains.'

The elder announced that he had no objection to the request as put forward.

'Let the girls of this clan come in and greet the visitors.'

And there filed in a string of elderly women of the clan modestly dressed in *busuuti* of subdued colours, aunts and wives of older sons of the clan and wrinkled grandmothers. They knelt on a straw mat in front of the visitors and warmly greeted them.

'Is she one of them?' asked the elder, suppressing a smile at his own trickery.

'No, no! These are wonderful, elegant and time-tested ladies of the clan, but our dream one is not among them.'

The spokesman sent away the not-so-young and elderly ladies and called for any remaining young women of the clan to come in.

And there walked in, attired in bright little dresses, toddler girls and small girls many seasons away from beginning to sprout tiny swellings on their chests, to the amazement of the visitors and giggles of the hosts. The toddler girls and small girls knelt on the mat and piped their soprano greetings to the guests.

The spokesman and the rest of his party simply gaped and then hilariously laughed their utmost at this piece of theatrical performance by their resourceful hosts.

'I can see that you're not impressed by this age-group of our female population. Go back, dear girls. And next let's have whatsoever remaining girls there are to come and greet the visitors.'

And there stepped in, one by one, the choice remnant of the clan's women, radiant grown-up beauties draped in superior silken *busuuti* of a golden hue, who each seemed without compare. They knelt on the mat and melodiously chorused their greetings to the visitors.

'Is she among these last comers?' asked the elder, with a knowing smile playing on his face.

'Ye-ye-yes, elder!' stammered the spokesman. 'Yes, elder, she is among them. I see her, I see her!'

'Well then,' calmly continued the elder, 'can you point her out?'

'Yes, sir, I can,' the spokesman enthused. 'Yes, elder, I can, if you'll allow me.'

'Go right ahead and do exactly that.'

While the eyes of every host were glued on the spokesman not to miss his imminent steps, a young woman from Mwambu's entourage suddenly got up, and then un-wrapped a parcel from a paper box that she had been holding on her lap all along. It was a bouquet of flowers; and smartly walking with it to the clan beauties still kneeling on the mat, she knelt down before Nakintu and gave it to her.

Applause from every guest and host and ululations from the hosting womenfolk were heard.

'Well, well, well!' the elder called out with an animated face. 'And now it's your turn, Nakintu our dear daughter,' he continued, 'to point out the young man from among these visitors who would like to steal you away from this home.'

All eyes fixed on Nakintu as she elegantly rose to her feet, only to be instantly diverted by the sudden emergence from the main house of an elderly lady of regal bearing, Nakintu's paternal aunt, dressed in a purple *busuuti* of exquisite quality and carrying a wreath. She walked straight to Nakintu, stopped next to her, and the two steadily progressed side by side with the proud and happy show-off of pea-hens towards the semi-circle of the visitors. They approached five of the men in the visiting entourage who at that material moment feigned sleepiness, with their drooping heads apparently trying to avoid being recognised. One by one, the elderly lady jacked up the drooping heads, from the first to the third, till she spotted in the forth drooping head – the face of Mwambu. Quickly, she passed on the wreath to Nakintu, who immediately knelt before Mwambu and coyly put it around his neck.

There was applause, ululations, a rumble of mighty drums, and many other ecstatic sounds.

When the happy sounds gradually died down, the spokesman once more stood up and begged the elder to further indulge him by way of allowing him to perform one final modest duty. In response, the elder announced that the permission was freely given there and then.

'Our marvellous, honourable, and magnanimous hosts,' the spokesman proceeded, 'we would like to express our most hearty gratitude to you, owners of this homestead and offspring of this clan, for allowing our family to be joined to your family in a blood relationship. We're gaining the daughter you seem to be losing; and you're gaining the son we seem to be losing.

'And now it is my singular privilege and pleasure to request you to please accept from us your guests, who were but a short while ago total strangers from an unknown land, a handful of presents and tokens to various members of your family – as an expression of our appreciation and love for you.'

Taking their cue from the spokesman, young men and women previously alerted for the purpose swiftly moved to the pick-up truck and made several trips of bringing in the colourfully wrapped gifts – the females expertly balancing the gifts in straw baskets upon their heads, and the males bearing boxfuls of gifts in both hands and holding them close to their bellies. They comprised assorted items of foodstuffs for general consumption and various pieces of attire with labels of specific recipients – the bride-to-be, parents, grandparents, uncles, aunties, brothers and cousins.

'The very last gifts,' the spokesman cheerfully called out, 'are of a somewhat special kind and a special meaning for us. They include, as you can see while they come in one by one –

'Mountain bamboo shoots, both smoked and fresh, a dinner delicacy which, we hope, you may find to be far more delicious than any lowland mushrooms;

'Mountain yams of the perennial *tsimbama* and *bikhwa* species which, we trust, you will eat and savour to the very tips of your fingers and toes;

' A garment of home-treated soft cow-hide, for our father of the house, the Reverend Kintu, perhaps to wear on top of his *kanzu* or his cassock whenever he comes visiting us up there in the land of clouds ; –'

Giggles and open laughter from both sides.

'A home-crafted medium-length skirt, that has been in fashion since ancestral times,' continued the spokesman with tongue-in-cheek glee, 'made from threads out of banana stems, for our mother of the house, *Mukyala* Mary, perhaps to also wear on a similar visit on top her *busuuti;* –'

Spontaneous laughter all around.

'And the last token of them all,' said the spokesman in an even more jovial tone, 'which the Reverend and our mother may wish to place in some corner of their sitting-room – is a circumcision knife –'

'What!' chorused the hosts in a mixture of amusement and shock.

'Yes,' he asserted with a semi-serious grimace, 'this is in token that, in obedience to our ancient rite of manhood, all males born of the imminent union between the daughter of this clan and the son of our clan shall be circumcised.'

'No problem, no problem!' shouted the elder jumping to his feet. 'That's no problem at all,' he cheerfully repeated.

'The only problem I can see at this very historic moment,' he warmly continued, tactfully changing the subject, 'is that you our long-distance guests must be starving by now. Because we've been feeding you on air since you arrived. So I hereby declare that three things be done in quick succession.

'The third one is going to be –'

'The *third* one or the *first*?' audibly queried a boy's voice from among the musicians' group.

'The *third* one, yes – that's what I said, my dear young one! The third one is going to be a late lunch for both guests and hosts.

'The *second* one is going to be a time of cross-greetings, when hosts and guests may freely exchange greetings and get to know one another.

'And the *first* thing is going to be a musical interlude.

'And now let the instruments speak. Let the musicians serenade this day, and let costumed dancers break forth into jubilation craze. Come on, instruments...Come on, tuneful singers...Come on, long drums, pipes, flutes, xylophones, rattles and horns!'

So the music broke out. A festivity song of *Nankasa* species hit and electrified the air. From opposite directions suddenly materialised two files of dancers, one comprising women and one comprising men, who zestfully stormed the dance arena: the women in sleeveless yellow blouses, broad ankle-length brown-red-and-orange cotton-cloth wrappers with horizontal stripes, and black goat-skins tied over their well-pronounced posteriors as rhythmic amplifiers; the men naked from the shoulders to the waist, wearing strong khaki shorts, white sisal wrappers over their behinds, and bands of rattles over their legs; men and women at their most elegant upon bare feet, and nimbly performing upon the tips of those practiced feet in a from-the-waist-downwards dance of celebration frenzy; the men and the women each on their own in a single formation or in pairs, followed by ever-changing formations of one-man-to-one-woman in provocative, suggestive wriggles and gyrations; one steady movement followed by a rigorous one; one relaxed movement followed by a vigorous one; now every duo seductively jiving towards each other, then proudly prancing away from each other in a story of yes-and-no wooing, rejection and acceptance – and all the movements and all the singers and all the instruments and all the dancers increasingly waxing in unison to an ecstatic climax, to a statement of peak orchestral happiness, and terminating in rapturous applause.

'Well done! Well done!' the elder excitedly called out. 'Well done and thank you! Thank you, dancers. Thank you, singers. Thank you, players upon the instruments. And thank you to all makers of musical instruments here and everywhere.

'And now,' he announced with a satisfied gesture of both hands, 'let's proceed to our last but one item – greetings and interaction.'

* * *

On arrival of his party into the compound of the Reverend and his wife, Mwambu had, to his utter amazement, immediately recognised one face among the hosts. Throughout all the subsequent speeches and activities, he had been wondering to himself what an incredible coincidence this was. And now with the opportunity created for greeting around, he zigzagged his way to the owner of the one face he had twice encountered before.

'Mr. Muntu,' Mwambu called, 'what a surprise to meet you here!'

'Oh, is it?' Muntu returned with a knowing smile. 'Don't they say that this world is round?'

'This conclusively confirms that it is,' Mwambu joked back. 'But I seem to remember from what you said before that you're not of the clan of the Kintus.'

'That's right. I'm of the Elephant clan.'

'And that's what I remember. So how come you might be my future uncle-in-law?'

'Ah, the answer is simple,' Muntu replied.

'How simple?'

'Very simple. I was invited to this occasion as a *musangi* of the Reverend Kintu – our wives are sisters.'

'Aha!' Mwambu aspirated. 'So you're the husband of Nakintu's Auntie Nnaalongo, the mother of twins!'

'That I am,' Kintu confirmed.

'Then I must henceforth address you,' Mwambu enthused, half wondering about this new dimension, 'as Uncle Ssaalongo, the father of twins.'

'Not really. I prefer that you call me Muntu we Butonda.

'I shall do that. I shall do that, Uncle Muntu we Butonda.'

But Mwambu's brain was already in a spin. And it continued to spin through the final item of the day's agenda, the late lunch...*What coincidences! This Muntu I meet on my first journey to the plains...is a Ssaalongo, father of twins, who prefers not to be known as such...as if he was not one, or is not one...and the two sisters...one married to a priest of Jesus Christ, one married to a high priest of Katonda we Butonda, the keeper of the shrine of the Creator of Creation Place... and Nakintu and I are supposed to be part of this jig-saw puzzle...part of what I don't know...part of what she doesn't know...or does she?...*

* * *

'Go well, our visitors. Go well, and come back soon... for a different reason...'

'Stay well, our hosts and hostesses. Stay well, and see you again very soon...when we come to pick the hoe for our handle that is without a hoe...'

XIV
Therefore Shall a Man Leave his Parents

Three moons later Mwambu and Nakintu became man and wife. One hour after the bridegroom and his best man Lwanga in their black suits with white shirts, striped black-and-white neckties and black pointed shoes had punctually occupied their seats for the nuptial ceremony at noon in the imposing Namirembe Cathedral, proud seat of the Native Anglican Church in the land, the glamorous bridal group trailed in, Nakintu draped in flowing immaculate white from top to toe, her matron in a purple long dress and shoes of similar hue, and her retinue of six bridesmaids in knee-high pink dresses with low-cut backs and matching maroon high heels.

Here comes my bride, thought Mwambu, mesmerised as Nakintu and her matron drew alongside him and stopped in front of the priest. Loud, accelerated drumbeats struck up in the insides of both bridegroom and bride, as they took in scarcely a word of the priest's usual pious introductory remarks. And then –

'...First, it was instituted for the procreation of children...' And Mwambu's charged brain cut in, *Ah, but long before this have I started on that.*

'...Secondly, it was instituted as a remedy against sin...' *Such as I have known, O Lord, in a married woman's bed –*

'...Thirdly, it was instituted for mutual companionship, so that the one ought to have of the other...' *No marriage, no companionship? -*

'...Into which holy estate Abraham Mwambu and Sarah Nakintu come now to be joined. Therefore if any man or woman can show any just cause why they may not be lawfully joined together –'

Nakintu shivered and tensed up as Mwambu's queer question on her very first visit to his student room flashed on an invisible screen before her – *Or is baby crying at home?*

'...Let him speak it now...'

And in a twinkling Mwambu figured, *Suppose some crazy rogue came bursting in from the back shouting that he was her first lover, and that from the time he first bedded her –*

'...or be forever silent.'

Mwambu and Nakintu involuntarily exchanged furtive enigmatic smiles.

'With this ring I thee wed, with my body I honour thee, and with all my worldly goods I thee endow...'

Rings of gold, bodies of honour, and goods of endowment, Mwambu silently intoned.

'... Abraham Mwambu and Sarah Nakintu, I pronounce you man and wife.'

Ululations burst out from grandmothers, aunts and sisters; there were

loud drum-strokes of delight in breasts of relatives and friends.

And Mwambu's bubbling inside said – *Clap; clap your hands, you angels above! Clap; clap your hands, spirits of the ever-living dead!*

'And what God has put together, let no man or woman put asunder!'

Here and there in the congregation, worldly-wise men smiled cynical smiles of just-you-wait-and-see.

*   *   *

The first night of the couple's honeymoon, spent at the cozy and tranquil Kampala Lakeside Inn, was dutifully supervised by Ssenga, Nakintu's paternal aunt. Upon Nakintu's insistence days before, that she would need a senior aunt around her for the first night, Mwambu had had a room reserved for Ssenga in advance, just three doors away on the same corridor as the bridal guest room. After dinner, when the couple was preparing to retire to their bridal bed, Mwambu told Nakintu to send Ssenga to her room.

'But, Abby, she's going to sleep with us in our room,' announced Nakintu.

'What!' exclaimed Mwambu.

'Yes,' Nakintu coolly replied. 'That's why she's Ssenga.'

'What do you mean by that? Is there something I haven't understood?'

'It seems so. Your best-man should have explained to you.'

'Explained to me what, Sarah?'

'That Ssenga must share our room with us on our first night together.'

'Spirits of the mountains! And sleep *between* us?'

'No, it's not that bad,' Nakintu coyly replied. 'Not between us but *near* us.'

And so it was that after much puzzling out of the purpose and implications of Ssenga's mission to the honeymoon chamber, Mwambu begrudgingly consented to Ssenga's overnight presence in the room. Accordingly, Nakintu had an extra mattress brought in by the assistant innkeeper for Ssenga and placed on the floor in a corner. And while Mwambu and Nakintu shyly got into their bed in the dimmed light, Ssenga also snugly lay down on her mattress and readied herself to stay awake to generally oversee her niece's first marital night.

A few heartbeats later, Ssenga started feeling ripples of delight mixed with anxiety. She remembered the time, many seasons back, when she had led Nakintu, along with her teen age-mates, to the bush to perform anatomical modification upon their secret regions into the future pride of their womanhood. As she pondered these things, her mind swung back to the present reality of witnessing her niece's passage from being a single young woman to a wife. Then, with increased anxiety, she suddenly wondered why she had not yet heard any sound of life. For an instant, she contemplated that last resort of an exasperated Ssenga: of practically taking Mwambu over from her niece and demonstrating to her how to conduct the nuptial rite.

Meanwhile, Mwambu was experiencing extreme nervousness to the point of temporary impotence before his long-awaited bride. The mere thought of a third presence in his bridal room simply unmanned him. Sensing this, Nakintu called up all the seductive expressions that she had lately rehearsed to perfection, but which now sounded like coming from somewhere deep in her interior, thereby slowly coaxing Mwambu into some minimal desire in spite of himself:

> Master and lover of my heart...
>
> You're dynamite beyond compare...
>
> You're the pioneer warrior of the mountains...
>
> You're the victorious invader of the plains...
>
> You're the vanquisher of the un-conquerable...
>
> All the flowers in the valleys are yours...
>
> All the beehives on the hillsides are yours...
>
> You're the governor of all my dominions...
>
> All the territories of Buganda are yours ...

'That's right! That's the spirit!' Ssenga breathed to herself, nodding and beaming with the supra satisfaction of a tutor who had done an excellent job. And she soon drifted off into a carefree slumber.

*   *   *

With the first rays of the sun filtering through the curtains, Nakintu eased out of bed, wrapped a towel around her and went to the bathroom. Opening his eyes on his bride disappearing behind the bathroom door, Mwambu also got out of bed, slid into his nightgown and followed her.

Within a twinkling, Ssenga was on her feet. She made a straight line for the bridal bed, threw back the blanket and top bed-sheet, and her eyes fell on what she and Nakintu had connived to ensure – a blood stain in the centre of the bottom bed-sheet. In order for the mother-bride to pass for a virgin on her nuptial night, Ssenga had hatched the little scheme that the wedding day should fall in the very middle of her niece's visit to the moon.

When Nakintu and Mwambu amorously walked back from the bathroom, Ssenga was smartly sitting up on her mattress. And the bridal bed still had the blanket and top bed-sheet thrown back for the couple to know that Ssenga had seen what she had seen. She smiled a knowing smile at them as they got back into bed and covered themselves with the dishevelled top bed-sheet and blanket.

By mid morning Ssenga was on her way back to her home in the village. On account of the blood stain on her niece's bridal bed-sheet, she was the automatic beneficiary of a choice she-goat, as a token of appreciation for her having safeguarded Nakintu's virginity. But the more she reduced the distance between her and home, the more did Ssenga wonder if she should accept that she-goat when sent to her.

XV
Enter the Nephew

On their first visit to Mwambu's parents' home, bride and groom caused a stir among the villagers. For the groom was the first to bring a stranger woman home, one from the very end of the world. And the bride fitted this picture very well by having almost every bit of conversation translated for her by the groom apart from the simplest greeting.

But everyone said that she was very beautiful and pleasant and that she would learn the mountain tongue with time and with some input from Mwambu.

And in response to the visits of felicitations from the neighbours, Mwambu took his bride on a number of return visits to his friends and kinsfolk. The third visit took the couple to the home of Mwambu's cousin Kuloba and his wife Mayuba. At the material time Kuloba happened to be away at a neighbour's house, and so it was Mayuba who received the newly-wed guests.

'On whom are my eyes falling!' she exclaimed in pure delight, getting up and stepping out from the veranda.

'They are falling on us,' Mwambu replied as cheerfully.

'Come, come,' she directed, opening out her arms; 'let me squeeze you tight with a hug, you our darling husband; and you with another, my most welcome sweet co-wife!'

Fifteen years on, thought Mwambu with a regretful internal shake of the head, *and she hasn't changed a bit! Fifteen years gone by since she overwhelmed, overpowered, and swept me into her bed – with incredible human outcome.*

'Welcome you both,' she continued, indicating two of the folding wooden chairs on the veranda to the left of the door. 'Thank you, husband of ours, for bringing home my competitor for your love. Tell her, tell her, Mwambu my own husband from long ago, how very welcome she is to the homestead of many wives.'

Nakintu asked Mwambu to interpret the seemingly happy words of welcome.

'She's expressing her joy as hostess,' Mwambu summarised, 'with sentiments that echo memories of bygone times.'

'Tell my young and dearest co-wife,' Mayuba fervently carried on, seating herself on one of the spare folding chairs to the right of the door, 'of the competitions awaiting her: of how the love of our man, your love, is going to be won and sustained through the peeling knife, the grinding-stone, the black cooking-pot, and the millet brew-pot.'

Again Nakintu asked Mwambu to interpret.

'She's speaking in metaphors about love as feeding on the kitchen, and on home-made millet brew which –'

'Ah, but here comes my elder husband,' announced Mayuba, mustering a special smile and straightening up in her seat.

And for sure, Kuloba made the bend in the path to the right side of the house and immediately came into direct view of his wife and the guests.

'Child of my father and our bride!' he excitedly called out on seeing bride and groom.

'Elder child of my father!' warmly reciprocated Mwambu, respectfully standing up.

The two struck hands in a hearty greeting. Kuloba gave an equally hearty handshake to Nakintu. He then sat down on the chair which Mayuba vacated to go busy herself in the kitchen boiling water for a pot of millet brew.

Addressing Mayuba by her pet-name, Kuloba gaily called across the yard, 'NaButiilu, what are you going to slaughter for our rare guests? A she-goat or bull-buffalo?'

'An elephant is what I suggest;' Mayuba merrily shouted back, 'an animal huge enough for us all to feast upon and celebrate for a whole moon.'

'That's right. But you first hurry up with something to warm the bellies.'

Mayuba duly produced a mini clay-pot half-full of bubbling millet brew from the main house. She topped up the pot with a calabash of boiling water to the brim, and handed to Kuloba the thin wooden pipe containing the drinking tube. He pulled the tube out of the pipe, placed it into the millet brew pot, made a good number of initial suction pulls at the tube as host, and passed it on to Mwambu. After a few pulls, Mwambu in turn ceremonially passed the tube on to Nakintu as chief guest for a more prolonged suction effort. She did her best at the maiden exercise but shyly passed the tube on to Kuloba after no more pulls than the fingers on her hand.

'This is called telephoning heaven, bride of ours,' jovially remarked Kuloba to Nakintu as the communion tube circled back to him. 'It's sending a long-distance message to God and the ancestors – through this pliable wooden cable – that life is good, and thanking them for the many uses of millet.'

Mwambu translated for Nakintu.

'That's wonderful,' she radiantly replied. 'I mean the idea of telephoning other worlds through the drinking-pot! But what are the many uses of millet?'

'I think I've understood her LuGanda there,' said Kuloba. 'One use is the one we're participating in right now.'

'That's one,' Mwambu prompted Kuloba, after interpreting for Nakintu.

141

'Two is feeding the dregs of the brew-pot to the chickens.'

'That's two.'

'Three is millet grains directly fed to the chickens.'

'Three.'

'Four is pouring libation on the graves of the ancestors.'

'Four.'

'Five is, of course, food; it's food in various forms – solid *ugali* for the adults, and watery porridge for the little ones.'

'Five.'

'Six is *kamamela,* yeast for fermenting the millet brew.'

'Six.'

'Seven is *limela*, the yeast paste for smearing on the bodies of circumcision initiates.'

'Seven.'

'Eight is *kamayeku,* the sweet unfermented drink for teetotallers and freshly circumcised candidates.'

'Eight.'

'Nine is sowing the grain in the soil for the next harvest.'

'Nine.'

'And many, many more uses!'

'That's Ten-plus-plus! And many, many more uses!' intoned Mwambu with an inflexion of finality.

'Wow, wow!' interjected Nakintu. 'Maybe the list is endless! It sounds like the mystery grain of the mountain.'

'It's like – for you medics – your multi-purpose aspirin, I would say,' observed Mwambu in rejoinder.

Meanwhile Kuloba was hatching an idea that he had been incubating for many, many moons in closed consultation with Peter Wayelo the long-time rival of Mwambu, and with the consent of Wopata the unrelenting bitter circumcision-mate of Masaaba. Now seemed the moment most propitious to bring it up.

'Wandayase, child of the same womb,' he called, using the pet-name by which male cousins love to address each other.

'Yes, Wandayase,' replied Mwambu interestedly.

'There's something I've been meaning to ask of you for these passing moons. It's a kind of favour. But then, a favour to one's kin is like a favour to one's own self, isn't it?'

'I guess so,' replied Mwambu with a sense of curiosity. 'But what is it? Can I hear it at once?'

'Of course you can, Wandayase. It's about our son Ishmael Buwayilila.'

'Oh, is it?' asked Mwambu with a tinge of apprehension. *Our son, you say?*

'Yes, it is. You see, he's now in the eighth year of school, in Junior Secondary Two at Namwombe. You know that there's now a secondary school at Namwombe, don't you?'

'Yes, I do. But does he have a problem there?'

'No, not a problem. It's just that I've been thinking about asking you to help him get into a good secondary school in Kampala after the end of this year, if he passes to join Senior Secondary. If possible, I would like him to stay with you and our young wife at your house, and daily walk to school from there.'

'But there are good schools around here – Elgonton, for instance, where I received a quite good education. Why would you want him in Kampala?' *What a difficult thing to ask for! Why, why? Sarah won't like it. Anothers' child to be the first under our roof!*

'It's for a very good reason. I want you to mould him into a very clever student. I also want him to grow up knowing that we're a large clan, and that he has many fathers –'

'What!' *Jesus, what's he driving at?*

'Yes, he should know that he has many fathers, or at least two – you and I.'

'Yes, yes, Wandayase,' Mwambu impatiently agreed. 'But Buwayilila must be knowing all this.'

'In fact, with my poor village means that cannot take him far, I wish that he should regard me as his second father, and –'

My God, my God! 'What are you saying, Kuloba?' Mwambu was getting exasperated.

'And that he should regard you as his first father.'

'What are you two talking about?' Nakintu butted in, sensing Mwambu's rising agitation.

'Oh, it's some issue of an educational nature,' he explained with as much control of his feelings as he could, 'within the extended family. He's asking the two of us for a small but somewhat difficult favour. I'll put you in the picture later this evening.'

Then calmly but resolutely turning to Kuloba, he said, 'Wandayase, don't you think that we've looked on you enough for one day?'

'Not quite, Wandayase,' Kuloba replied with raised, questioning eyebrows. 'What are you suggesting?'

'I'm saying that we've visited you for a very good while, and we would like to leave now.' He gave an eye message to Nakintu to get up.

'But I'm sure,' Kuloba protested in apparent disbelief at his guests' being already on their feet, 'that we were just beginning to telephone the ancestors.'

'Ah, but don't they say', Mwambu replied, grinning with one side of his mouth, 'that it's better to leave while you're still welcome?'

'And they also say,' Kuloba quickly countered, 'that if you see your guests off, they don't come back soon. So I'm not getting up to see you off. Go well, Wandayase.

144

And come back soon. And please remember my request!'

'Yes, I will.' *Yes, I will – you're hounding me, O God!* 'Yes, I will. Stay well, elder son of my father.'

'Go well, our youngest wife.'

Nakintu curtsied and waved to Kuloba in good-bye.

'Stay well, mother of the house,' Mwambu blankly called to Mayuba across the yard.

'No, you can't be leaving so soon!' Mayuba shouted back, stepping out of the kitchen. 'What has happened? I was just about to skin the elephant for the feast!'

'I'm afraid you'll have to skin it on our next visit. We have to call on another family before dark.'

'Oh, must you? Well then, go well,' she said with a sulky face. 'Go well, my younger husband.'

And there she goes! There she goes all over again!

'And go well, my youngest co-wife and sweetest rival.'

*   *   *

Buwayilila moved to Kampala to stay with the Mwambus at the beginning of the following year. By the time he started senior secondary school, he had already settled in his new home.

Coming from the mountain background, where no word exists distinguishing a man's sons from those of his brothers and his paternal cousins – Mwambu generally introduced Buwayilila to the visitors as a son of the house.

'Is he your real son,' asked one visitor, 'or just a nephew?'

'There's no such thing,' Mwambu promptly answered, 'as real sons and unreal ones. Do you mean to say that what you call nephews are *unreal* sons?'

'You know what I meant, Mwambu. I simply wanted to know if he is your biological child.'

'That's not as simple,' Mwambu quibbled, 'as you think. In my culture, a child is not born to a particular

145

couple but to the whole clan, to the community. This, in reality, makes your so-called biological fathers merely adoptive fathers.'

'And what do you mean by that?'

'That Buwayilila is as much my son as he is that of his other father within the clan.'

'And that makes you sound,' observed the puzzled visitor, 'too clever by half, Mwambu.'

XVI
Enter the Niece

After their wedding, the Mwambus had moved into the groom's ground-floor flat on Nakasero hill on a block of flats set aside for indigenous public servants of clerical and officer grades. The bungalows with their spacious compounds, exclusively occupied by British officials and the foreign business class, remained a dream of the future for the local pioneers graduating from the colleges.

One afternoon, when their marriage had lasted for as many moons as there are fingers on both hands and Nakintu was heavy with new life, Mwambu returned to the flat to find her in labour pains. He rushed her to hospital at once.

Way back before Nakintu became pregnant, the couple had agreed that if their first born was a baby girl, they would name her NaBarwa, after the mother of all Mwambu's mountain people; and if it was a baby boy, they would name him Kundu, after his ancestor who vanished from the mountain in the direction of the setting sun long, long ago.

Secretly, however, Nakintu was hoping that the first baby she bears for Mwambu would be a boy, an inheritor of paternal estates. And as secretly, Mwambu was hoping for a girl, just to have the pleasure of contradicting the village mentality that regarded a baby girl coming first as poor luck for the father, having been convinced way back during his catechism classes prior to his baptism as a young boy that children of either sex are equal gifts from the Creator.

It therefore came as a real surprise for both the young parents and their doctor when the midwife delivered Nakintu of two babies within minutes of each other, a girl and a boy.

'Congratulations, Nnaalongo!' the midwife exuded. 'Congratulations, mother of twins!'

Nakintu, who had been commanded to push and push all over again after her first baby came out, smiled with a mixture of pain, relief, wonderment and gratification that bordered on the sublime.

The midwife radiated her congratulations at Mwambu as he was finally permitted into the labour ward from the waiting room.

'Congratulations, Ssaalongo! You've got a baby boy and a baby girl.'

'I-I-I be-be-beg your pardon,' stammered Mwambu.

'I'm saying well done, you enviable father of twins!'

'My God, my God, I can't believe this!' *Both Kundu and NaBarwa at once!*

'You had better believe what your eyes are seeing, you learned, doubting Thomas,' the midwife joked, leading him to his wife and the twins.

'Don't twins run in your family?' the midwife asked Mwambu.

'Oh, yes, they do – some generations back. But hardly ever as the first time that you become a father!' *Bly me, I'm no first-time!*

'And in yours?' she asked Nakintu.

'I'm not sure,' she moaned. 'Bu-bu-but, on my mother's side, yes. My mother's younger sister married in Kyaggwe,' *but God you know that this is not true*, she agonised in ambiguous pain, 'is Nnaalongo.'

'Well, then,' concluded the midwife, 'neither of you should be so astonished at your good luck – which comes to about one in fifty couples.'

*   *   *

'Come, let us dance the twins!' shouted one overjoyed woman from the next-door flat on the ground floor.

'Yes,' another woman from a flat on the second floor concurred, 'come all you fellow women of the neighbourhood, and let us dance the birth of twins!'

'Let us sing and dance for the twins who have chosen to belong to our locality.'

'But first, let us ask Nnaalongo a question or two. Were the twins born in this flat of yours or in that small banana grove below the flats – with you holding onto a banana stem as you pushed the babies into the world?'

'They were born in neither place. They were born in Mulago Hospital.'

'So were they born for you, or did you give birth to them yourself? I ask because I hear that in hospital they sometimes cut you open to get the babies out, instead of letting you give birth normally.'

'No, no, no – I gave birth to them myself.'

'But who acted as your *Mulelwa*, to deliver the babies – and to proclaim their arrival?'

'It was some kind woman, a midwife, who I had never seen before.'

'How then were the twins allocated to the sexes?'

'Yes, tell us. Was baby boy's umbilical cord cut with a spear, to signify his manhood?'

'And was baby girl's umbilical cord cut with a knife or a hoe, to signify her womanhood?'

'No, both umbilical cords were cut with a pair of scissors.'

'Ah, what terrible change has befallen us there!'

'All the same, let the babies be named with the going down of the sun, that in the morning they may germinate with the new sun.'

'Yes, you Ssaalongo there: in the absence of an elder from your clan, you give the twins their names.'

First taking one twin into his arms and then the other, as if he had rehearsed it all before, Mwambu in turn ceremonially intoned from somewhere deep inside him:

> You, my fellow man, I give you the names of Kundu Wasswa Mukhwana, double names of the male older twin. And since you're the first born, I also give you the name of Kigongo, the elder sibling of twins, who carries the twins upon his back. Grow up as a good person: wise, generous, truthful and hardworking.

> You, mother of all clans, I give you the names of NaBarwa Nnakato Namono. NaBarwa of the double names of the female younger twin, you first mother of my mountain race, grow up as a hardworking woman: kind and fair in judgement.

And then the women took over. To Mwambu, who gaped hyptonised, these women of the plains seemed to have long practiced their lines, and now only needed to insert his new title and that of Nakintu. The song leader sang each successive line, and all the others repeated it.

> And now let us dance for you,
> Ssaalongo and Nnaalongo;
> Let us sing and dance for you,
> Wasswa Mukhwana and Nnakato Namono.
> Let us sing and dance to you the song and dance
> Of gender, love and procreation;
> Come, all you nearby men and women,
> Come, let us gyrate and jive in jubilation –
> Let us enact the seductive dance of life!

Next, singing in unison, they broke into one of the ancient songs of the plains for twins.

Nanyinimu, tolaba bwenkola	Head of the house, don't see what I do
Kigongo Ssaalongo…	Elder Sibling and Father of Twins…
Tolaba bwenkola	Don't see what I do
Kigongo bbale	*O Elder Sibling of Twins*
Nanyinimu, tolaba bwenzina	Head of the house, don't see how I dance
Kigongo Ssaalongo…	Elder Sibling and Father of Twins…
Tolaba bwenzina	Don't see how I dance
Kigongo bbale	*O Elder Sibling of Twins*
Nanyinimu, tokuba kubaana	Head of the house, don't beat the children
Kigongo Ssaalongo…	*Elder Sibling and Father of Twins…*
Tokuba kubaana	Don't beat the children
Kigongo bbale	*O Elder Sibling of Twins*
Nanyinimu, weeryowe	Head of the house, calm down
Tuleeta Ssaalongo	We are bringing Father of Twins
Weeryowe	Calm down
Tuleeta abalongo bo	We are bringing your twins
Kigongo bbale	*O Elder Sibling of Twins*

Their impromptu performance over, the women and their men made themselves generally feel at home in the sitting room and kitchen, on the veranda and the grass, and merrily partook of drinkables and edibles hastily improvised by their excited and overwhelmed host and hostess.

* * *

But within the first moon of her being Mother of Twins, Nakintu experienced the unforeseen demands of double breastfeeding, double changing of nappies, and catching mere snatches of sleep in the night, notwithstanding Mwambu's committed support and the routine chores of Nnanteza, the elderly female house worker. It therefore became very clear that she needed a second house help.

'Mwambu,' she called her husband by his favourite name, tenderly touching his arm as they drank their cup of tea one evening.

'Yes, Wife of my Youth, my Na-kintu, my Na-Object, my Female-Thingamabob,' he fondly replied.

By the end of the conversation, Nakintu had easily convinced Mwambu about the need for at least a part-time helper around the house.

'And it had better be a female,' Nakintu said. 'For, as you can see, we have Buwayilila but he's of little help when it comes to things like changing nappies. Not surprising, being the last born in his family, he had no nappies to change.'

'Do you have someone in mind?' Mwambu asked.

'Yes. I've been thinking about one of the twins of my mother's sister.'

'Ah, you mean Aunt Nnaalongo Muntu?'

'Yes. You remember the twins were two of our six bridesmaids. I'm rather fond of Cleopatra Nantongo, the one that people say resembles my mother and me.' *Careful – I should watch what I say!*

'Oh well, it's not surprising for first cousins to resemble each other, is it?'

'No, of course not. As a matter of fact, Cleo hardly calls me cousin or sister, but rather Maama, since I'm that much older than her.' *There I go again!*

'You're old enough to be her mother?' Mwambu innocently asked.

'What!' There was a tinge of panic and fright in her voice. *Gods of my ancestors! That insinuation!*

'Have I asked a silly question?' Mwambu was puzzled.

'No, not really,' she smiled reassuringly. 'Except that you should know that I'm not that old!' she proudly announced.

'Of course, I know,' he smiled back. 'You're only old enough to be a Nnaalongo – and much more.'

'There you go again!' *Sprits of Lake Nalubaale, he knows something.* 'What do you mean by my being much more?' *I really wonder about this Mwambu.*

'Nothing, nothing, I assure you, my sweet Nathingamabob!' he answered, stroking her arm. 'Let's agree as to when Nantongo joins us.'

'Yes, we better do that,' she said with a sigh of relief. 'You know that she has just sat Junior Secondary Leaving Examinations.'

'Yes, I do. Which means that she's at exactly the same stage Buwayilila was one year ago?'

'That's right. So she can come almost immediately. She too can attend senior secondary school around here in due course, but continue to be available to help me with the twins.'

'That's all right. But since she calls you Maama, should I address her as sister-in-law, niece or daughter?'

'Abraham!' she half-shouted, getting up and looking agitated. *Yes, he knows something!*

'I'm more than puzzled,' Mwambu protested. 'What's your problem?'

'I have no problem.' She shot back, walking away to the bedroom to apparently check on the twins. 'Maybe it's you having a problem. Call her what you want.'

'Goodness me!' Perplexed and angry, Mwambu got to his feet. 'Call her what I want? What utter nonsense! I'll call her what she is. She calls you Maama, so I'll simply call her daughter. But to the visitors, I'll of course be so British as to introduce her as my niece.'

XVII
Of Jobs and Vocations

'No going back!' proclaimed Lwanga over his frothy glass of Bell brew, Uganda's most popular lager, and referring to "the wind of change blowing across Africa" as quoted in a British daily. 'After Ghana, I say, there's no going back,'

'For sure, for sure,' Mwambu readily agreed, holding up and drinking from a similar glass. 'There can only be double acceleration towards the inevitable emancipation of mother Africa.'

The two were chatting away on the lower terrace of Kampala Empire Hotel, where they had converged to discuss an idea that Mwambu had been incubating for many moons.

'And so what is it,' Lwanga asked, 'that you hinted that you were going to announce to this august congregation of two eminent persons?'

'It's something that I've already discussed with Sarah, and that has met her approval. Which is that I'm quitting my job at Legco to –'

'You're doing what!' Lwanga was taken aback.

'I'm quitting my colonialist job.'

'For what good reason, Mwambu? Changing from your first job so fast, is that the beginning of your turning into a rolling stone?'

'No, not at all. I'll roll forward without becoming a stone.'

'It's good to hear that. But tell me why you're quitting.'

'I'm quitting a mere job,' Mwambu self-importantly declared, 'in order to take on a real vocation.'

'Oh, is there a difference?' Lwanga asked. 'Are you tired of working for pay and afraid of growing rich – and would therefore like to work for free, or rather for nothing?'

'That's not the point,' Mwambu replied. 'A vocation is not the same thing as volunteer work. It can even be work that pays very well. But whereas with a job you slave for the sake of the pay, with a vocation you do whatever work it is with satisfaction because of a sense of calling; because of the conviction that this is what you were created – and educated – to do.'

'Amen, Mr. Preacher-man!' Lwanga cheerfully teased. 'And what is this apparently pious calling of yours?'

'I would like to found and publish a newspaper.'

'What! And is that what you call a calling?'

'My answer is yes. And with your approval and help, I would like to do that on full-time basis.'

'You throw away your steady career for a newspaper! What kind of newspaper, if I may ask, and for what purpose?'

'A newsy newspaper, of course,' Mwambu naughtily replied.

'Oh yes,' conceded Lwanga, 'that's in so far as every newspaper carries some sort of report about new happenings. But what type of news will yours be?'

'Not of the usual kind of "man bites dog"; but something in the line of "black man gives white man a bleeding nose".'

'Well! I suppose that summarises the newspaper's purpose.'

'I hope so. I would like to inform and rally the reading as well as the non-reading masses to rise up and claim their political birthright from the usurper colonialists.'

'In that case, go right ahead.'

'Thank you. But I can only go ahead with your total support.'

'Do you want it in intellectual, physical, or metaphysical form?'

'I will want it in all those forms, and much more.'

'The much more,' Lwanga intuited, 'being that which appertains to the pocket?'

'Yes, yes, that,' Mwambu cheerfully nodded, 'and something else.'

'What something else?'

'That you'll please be a member of the editorial committee, will you?'

'That's no problem,' replied Lwanga. 'But what's to be the title of the paper?'

'*The People's Herald*,' was the ready answer.

'That sounds great! Long live the people!'

'And long live the newspaper,' Mwambu intoned with an air of achievement and satisfaction, 'that heralds the people!'

*　　*　　*

A good number are the fingers on both hands, and as many, less by two, were the political parties that sprung up like mushrooms in the closing years of the decade. Mwambu and Lwanga joined the Uganda Democratic Congress (UDC) on the grounds that it championed the control of the land and all productive sectors of the country by the central government for the common good of the people. At the extreme end of the political spectrum, and in direct opposition to UDC, there was the Traditional Landowners Party (TLP) that sought to safeguard the massive claims of the individuals owning large expanses of land, whether with squatters on them or not.

'In the free and new Uganda that we endeavour to create,' Mwambu wrote in an editorial of *The People's Herald*, 'we expect not only a democratic government

– of the citizens, by the citizens, for the citizens – but also a just economy, that benefits all the people in direct proportion to their reasonable needs, at the same time as each beneficiary should contribute his or her utmost to national wealth and to the overall wellbeing of the nation.'

*   *   *

The country was fast picking momentum towards forcing Britain to grant it its independence. Therefore at an opportune moment Mwambu decided to declare to his party executive committee his intention to contest for a parliamentary seat in his home constituency of Elgonton South. Thereafter, he interrupted his journalistic work from time to time to go on country-wide membership recruitment drives with the party's national campaign team, headed by its fiery president Hosea Hamilton Otebo, who was nicknamed Wamurwe – meaning "Big Head" in an Elgonian dialect – on account of his phenomenally long and wild head of hair. But because his three names started with H, H and O, to the school children throughout the country he was popularly known as H2O. And the head-boy at his former secondary school remarked at a school assembly that their school ancestor was politically as hot as when you burn a jet of hydrogen in a jar full of oxygen to manufacture water.

At a political rally in his own constituency of North Lakeside, party president Otebo, by now dangerously famous for his eloquent speeches, welcomed the party members who had travelled from various parts of the country.

'Fellow countrymen and countrywomen,' he called out in a rousing charismatic voice, 'I greet you in the name of freedom and unity. U-D-C!' he chanted, his open right hand raised way above his head, in his left hand holding his emblematic walking-stick.

'U-D-C!' the excited crowd yelled back.

'U-D-C!' he shouted again,

'U-D-C!' the crowd repeated.

'U-D-C!' he shouted a third time.

'U-D-C!' the crowd yelled at full throttle.

'E-very-where!' he chanted on, his body slightly dancing to his own voice.

'U-D-C!'

'E-very-body!'

'U-D-C!'

'Even you!'

'U-D-C!'

'Ah, ah, ah!'

'U-D-C!'

'Eh, eh, eh!'

'U-D-C!'

'Ih, ih, ih!'

'U-D-C!'

'Oh, oh, oh!'

'U-D-C!'

'Uh, uh, uh!'

'U-D-C!'

'Well done!' he enthusiastically bellowed with a downward turn of the voice. 'Well done, and a very warm welcome to everybody! What a great pleasure to see so many of us gathered together at this grand meeting in pursuit of our political birthright! Before I proceed, let me in a very special way welcome and recognise the presence of a truly significant number of eminent compatriots who have travelled from all corners of the country to grace this auspicious occasion. Please do stand up for recognition one by one as I call your name.'

Among the string of the proclaimed eminent names, Mwambu was most surprised to hear Otebo introduce '...Michael Musisi, the chief mobiliser of South-Central region...'

Michael Musisi all over again! Ubiquitous spirit, college drop-out, shrine custodian, political mobiliser...!

And because the names were being read in alphabetical order, immediately following upon Musisi, Otebo called out, '...Abraham Mwambu, the chief mobiliser of Elgonton South, and also chief editor of *The People's Herald*.'

Mwambu was up on his feet and up in the clouds. On resuming his seat, he did not hear the rest of the names of the eminent ones, until it came to the very final one.

'And last but not least,' Otebo called out, 'John Wambooza, the chief mobiliser of Elgonton North.'

The name fell like a heavy and hot echo from the distant past upon Mwambu's eardrums. Although he had never in person met the owner of that name, he was surely the elder cousin of his schooldays girlfriend, Nambozo of bitter memory. Now a full-grown woman in her early prime and a nursing officer in the government service, Nambozo was the one woman in the whole wide world that he hoped to never run into in his adult years. And neither did he wish to run into anyone or anything associated with her. But here now was someone in the shape of a fellow party mobiliser, one from the same Elgonton region at that, that he would have to rub shoulders with, or perhaps do worse than that...

'...In conclusion, fellow compatriots,' Mwambu, whose mind had ranged far and wide, finally heard Otebo say toward the very end of his speech, 'let me say this. In all our campaigns let's speak the same language. Let's remind our people that we're all one people, and we have a common goal, which is the independence of our country from the coloniser. Let there be no mention of Ugandans as Nilotic, Half Harmite, Nubian, or Bantu. Let's ensure that no linguistic, religious or cultural differences or diversities are permitted to undermine our unity.'

'Otebo oyee!' shouted an enthralled hero-worshipper from the swaying crowd.

'Oyee!' chorused the rest at the top of their voices.

'Otebo oyee!'

'Oyee!'

'Thank you, thank you!' responded Otebo in happy acknowledgement, once again raising his open right hand high above his head of long and wild hair. 'Thank you compatriots, and go well. And as you go, and when you get back to your various constituencies, persistently repeat our common message of freedom and unity. Repeat it to the towns and villages. Repeat it to the highlands and lowlands. Repeat it to the lakes and rivers. Repeat it to Mount Moroto, to Bufumbira Mountains, to the Mountains of the Moon in the west, to the Mountain of the Sun in the east...

And with that Mwambu caught his departure refrain! *Repeat it to the Mountains in the east... Repeat it to the Mountain of the Sun in the east...Repeat it...Repeat it...*

XVIII
Nephew and Niece

As he drove back home from the Lakeside North political rally, Mwambu was externally all bubbles, like millet brew on the second day after you sprinkle yeast upon its surface. And his interior was all ripples of delight.

When in the early afternoon he swung his Ford Cortina car into his compound, he instantly caught sight of Nakintu on the porch together with the twins, now aged three. Coming down the steps, Nakintu audibly shouted her welcome to Mwambu, while the twins scampered ahead of her upon their excited, light little feet.

'Papa yoyo!' Namono piped.

'Taata wuyo!' added Mukhwana

'Papa yoyo!'

'Taata wuyo!'

'That's Daddy!' they chorused in English. 'That's Daddy!'

'You wonderful, darling twins!' Mwambu ecstatically complimented them, crouching down and affectionately embracing them, one after the other. 'You're already speaking three languages at once!'

'Welcome back,' Nakintu said as Mwambu rose to his feet, and the two exchanged a prolonged warm hug.

'So happy to find you looking so good after these three days,' replied Mwambu, 'Nnaalongo, Wife of my Youth.'

'Looking good is one thing,' she remarked with the slightest hint of a frown. 'Feeling so is another.'

'Have you not been keeping well, my precious and priceless Thingamabob?' Mwambu asked with genuine concern in his voice.

But before she could reply, the twins imposed themselves on either side of Mwambu and each took charge of their father's nearer hand.

'Daddy, we go into the house,' Namono innocently commandeered, pointing towards the main door.

'And you tell us stories,' Mukhwana supplemented.

'OK, twins,' Mwambu consented. 'But the two of you walk ahead, while mummy and I follow.'

In the house, as soon as Mwambu sat down on the sofa, Namono placed herself on his right knee as Mukhwana placed himself on the left one, and they started to ask him one animated and philosophical question after another. Meanwhile their mum busied herself in the kitchen preparing tea and some bites in enough quantities for the whole lot of four that she had lately started calling the Mwambu Quartet.

*   *   *

During supper, Buwayilila and Nantongo being back from afternoon school, the family exchanged the usual daily pleasantries and non-pleasantries about town life in general. And in answer to Mwambu's question about school, Nantongo said that studies were going fairly smoothly.

'We're ponderating well under the atmospheric pressure,' added Buwayilila, wishing to show off some verbose lines he had recently picked from a book 'and are in a state of stable equilibrium, with nothing to disturb the morbosity.'

'Wow, Buwayilila!' Mwambu exclaimed while Nakintu frowned deeply. 'You're up to phenomenal tricks in linguistic gymnastics and acrobatics!'

'I think he's up to worse than that,' Nakintu cut in, quite nastily unlike her usual self.

'Oh, is he?' Mwambu quizzed, but received no answer from Nakintu while Buwayilila fidgeted uncomfortably.

The meal being over, the children went off to their beds after a short evening prayer: Nantongo to the room she shared with the twins and Buwayilila to his room on the servants' wing.

Remaining behind, Mwambu and Nakintu withdrew to the living room for a spell of relaxation. Again Mwambu asked Nakintu if she had not been feeling very well the past couple of days while he was away. Her answer was that indeed she had not, upon which he asked her what was amiss.

She replied with visibly disturbed silence.

'My Female-thing-one,' Mwambu coaxingly said, 'it appears that you would like me to have a guess at what problem there is.'

'No, it's not that,' she started to say, turning her back to Mwambu where they sat on the three-seat sofa.'

'Well, I assume it's not just your routine bad mood,' Mwambu tried joking, 'that you inflict upon me whenever the moon appears to you.'

'No, it's not!'

'Then what is it? Tell me!' Mwambu was getting quite exasperated. 'Or have you, on the contrary, missed sighting that heavenly sphere more than once and you're dreading the prospect of another by-product?'

'No! What has put that into your head? The real reason is that Buwayilila,' she blurted.

'Buwayilila? What has he done?' In a panicky flash Mwambu thought, *My God, has he made some teenage pass at his younger mother my wife?* 'What has the poor boy said or done to you?'

'*Done* to me?' Nakintu angrily asked, fighting off

165

possible sexual insinuation. 'He has said or done no rude or crude thing to *me*.'

'So then there's no problem, is that what you're saying?' He felt like giving her a sharp slap on the cheek to spout the words out of her.

'Yes, there is!'

'And that is what, you round-about woman?'

'Woman is what I am now, is that so?' she retorted, narrowing her eyes on him. 'How come you've never called me that before?'

'Because you have never before irritated me this much, the way some untutored country woman might do to her untutored country man!'

'Then let me tell you like the tutor-less woman I am,' she bitterly let out, 'that it is what that Buwayilila of yours has done to Nantongo.'

'And what has that Buwayilila of *mine* done to that Nantongo of *yours*?' Mwambu was enraged.

The mutual ambiguity of the possessive labels for Buwayilila and Nantongo made Nakintu sit up and shake her head. *My ancestors, how quick he is to hint that Nantongo is mine! Mine in what sense...?*

'And it's not the first time he does it to her,' she sulkily revealed.

'Go on,' he urged. 'It takes two to tangle, so the English saying goes. What have the two done?'

'You know Buwayilila has now been here for three years.'

'Yes, I sure know that.'

'And Nantongo has been here two years.'

'Yes, of course.'

'Well, I didn't want to tell you this the first time I suspected something. But within one month of Nantongo's coming to stay with us, I unexpectedly return from work one Saturday morning. I ask Nnanteza the baby-sitter where the two are, and she points to Buwayilila's closed room. I get to the room and turn the handle without knocking. The door is locked. I beckon to Nnanteza to come running and she does. I whisper to her to be the one to tell the two to open the door at once. She shakily does so, and the door opens – to reveal Nantongo in a terribly creased dress, her hair all in a mess! I pull her out, push the door wide open, and there on the bed was Buwayilila, pants off and his stupid little manhood so –'

'Enough!' Mwambu cut in. 'And you never told me?'

'No. Come this last Saturday it was very much the same thing, a repeat two years later. And this time I told myself I must tell you all about it.'

'Holy Jesus,' Mwambu cried out, putting his right hand across his eyes, 'what shame and disgrace!' *Like father, like son. Like uncle, like nephew. For I, the Lord your God, am a jealous God, visiting the sins of the fathers upon the children, unto the third and fourth generations...*

'And to think,' Nakintu went on, 'that they started when they were that young!' *And is that me expressing surprise, ancestors of my fathers...?*

'Not only that. It's not just that two teenagers are having sex; by our marriage, they're relatives.'

'That's right,' Nakintu agreed. 'Your nephew, who is as good as your son, is also a nephew and son to me and to my cousin.'

'Correct,' Mwambu concurred. 'And she is a cousin who is a child in our home, and therefore as good as a daughter of yours and mine.'

'Yes, it's as you say!' *There he goes with his double-sides words!*

'Therefore their having sex amounts to incest.'

'I agree with you. This is terrible!'

Mwambu sensed Nakintu was on the verge of emotional breakdown.

'Let me tell you this,' he said, shifting closer to her and holding her firmly in his arms. 'I actually have two measures in mind. First, I'm going to apply twelve muscular strokes of the cane to each of their behinds first thing in the morning. Secondly, I'm going to send them to same-sex boarding schools with strict instructions to their head teachers not to let them out of the school gates throughout the term.'

'And during vacations,' Nakintu added, wiping tears from her eyes, 'that Buwayilila must go back to his father Kuloba in the village.'

'Ah, but perhaps we should not move too fast. Let's decide where they spend their vacations at a later date. Otherwise I would also rush to rule that for the vacations Nantongo must go back to her mother, Aunt Nnaalongo, in the village.'

'All right,' Nakintu replied, finding it convenient to relent, 'let it be as you say.'

'Come, let's retire to bed,' Mwambu said as he got up, and felt weak all over. It was as if some ghost had drained his spirit and brain. He stretched his hands to Nakintu to help her get up. And then, to his utter surprise, as she heaved onto her feet holding onto his hands, he experienced unpredicted sudden eruption of sensuous desire for her.

'Come,' he repeated. Holding her right hand in his left, he led her into the corridor and on to their bedroom door. 'Come recreate for me the peak pleasures of our honeymoon, and make me forget today's revelations, before I awake to the politics and the harshness of everyday realities. Come unlock for me the infinite ecstasies of the plains.'

'Just as you ravish me,' she complemented with a dashing, seductive smile, 'with the glorious wonders of the mountains!'

XIX
I Take this Mountain and Eat it

After the North Lakeside political rally of UDC in Otebo's constituency, three months of intensive electioneering by all the parties culminated in the official nominations of parliamentary candidates countrywide. With all his qualification papers in order, Mwambu travelled to Elgonton three days ahead of time to avoid any last minute hitches that might deter him from beating the nomination deadline. And the nominations were scheduled to take place in the morning of the day following the final day of the campaigns. Polling day would be exactly seven days after nominations day.

Altogether, four different parties fielded candidates for Elgonton South. Of particular interest to Mwambu was his recent discovery that the campaign manager of one of the other three candidates fielded by that candidate's party, the Workers Unity Party (WUP), was the well-known talkative Second World War veteran, Peter Wayelo from Namisindwa sub-county, his classmate in the first year of primary school long ago at Namwombe Primary School and presently a clerk at Manafwa County headquarters. Only three days back, Mwambu had been shocked to learn that Wayelo had dubiously crossed from WUP to join UDC, the two of them thereby becoming members of the same party.

The night before the final electioneering day, which Mwambu spent at a hotel in Elgonton, he stayed awake for hours mentally going through the movements and major points he was to make the following afternoon in what was to be the climax of all his speeches.

Weighing his chances of beating his three opponents from the rival parties, he assured himself that his advantages were excellent. He also made a slight allowance for surprises – as occasionally happens in a game of soccer, or in the fireside game of posing and answering riddles.

'Ah, yes,' Mwambu thought aloud, 'the winner politician is like the soccer player, or the respondent to riddles. You can't predict the winner a hundred percent.'

His mind staying with riddles, he leapt the years backwards to his infant days by the fireside, with his father and mother posing riddles and answering them for him to hear and wonder, and he being unsure which of his parents would give the right answer to the next riddle. Oh, but how he marvelled at the clever objects that inhabited the riddles!

Father:	*Namunayi!*
	I send you a riddle!
Mother:	*Khupa kwitse.*
	Let it come.
Father:	*Ndi ni ngoko yase ikoneelela kamaki mu mawa.*
	I have this chicken of mine which incubates eggs among thorns.
Mother:	*Lulimi mu khanwa, l wayiboteekhelelwakameeno ne sikaluluma ta.*
	It is the tongue in the mouth, which is surrounded by teeth but they do not bite it.
Father:	*Nisy'e'syo! Waliile.*
	Correct! You have eaten.

Ah, but most memorable of all riddles was the one in which the largest object in the world was offered by his father to his mother to make her happy so that she could answer her own riddle.

Mother:	*Namunayi!*
	I send you a riddle!
Father:	*Khupa kwitse.*
	Let it come.
Mother:	*Ndi nu mwana wase; buli uwamayo ahambakho.*
	I have this baby of mine; whoever comes by takes his turn at holding it in his arms.
Father:	*Kumuharilo.*
	The peeling knife.
Mother:	*Taawe! Mb'endye ikhuboolele.*
	No! Give me a reward to eat and I tell you the answer.
Father:	*Nakhuhele ikhaafu ifuura bunere mwitaala lyefwe.*
	I give you the fattest cow in our kraal
Mother:	*Taawe! Iyo nakilobile, lwekhuuba singilya nekura ta. Mbe kundu kukali.*
	No! I reject that one, because I will not get satisfied after eating it. Give me something very big.
Father:	*Nakhuweele intsofu.*
	I give you an elephant.
Mother:	*Taawe! Iyo nayo nakilobile, lwekhuuba singilya nekura ta. Mbe sindu sifuura butsowu mu sibala syosi.*
	No! I reject that one also, because I will not get satisfied after eating it. Give me the loftiest thing in the whole world.

Father: *Nakhuweele lukingi Masaaba.*

I give you Masaaba's Mountain.

Mother: *Uryo---o! Nafukiilisile; ulwo kane indye
nikurire ilala, lwe bilayi bilulimwo bikali.*

Right! I accept; that one I will eat and
feel really full because of the many good
things therein.

*Ari khekuwe khukhwilibwamwo khwe
kumunayi. Umwana wase yesi buli
uwaamayo ahambakho nilyo lihakalo
mungo. Buli uwekumubano uba abira
ahakalilakho busa.*

And now let me tell you the answer to the
riddle. My baby that is held by whoever
comes by is the whet-stone in the
homestead. Every passer-by sharpens
his knife upon it for free.

Aya-ya-ya! Mwambu recalled how he went into
raptures. Eating the mountain! Being given the whole
mountain as reward and eating it! Gaining a whole
mountain because of knowing the riddle of the whet-
stone! Aya-ya-ya!

But what was it inside the mountain, he wondered,
that the solver of riddles, such as his clever mother,
would eat and get fully satisfied? What were the good
things inside it that were better than the meat of
cows and elephants, which his mother had rejected?
Was there some hidden sweetness beyond all other
sweetness perhaps somewhere deep down inside the
mountain...?

And then in his first year of primary school, Mwambu
and his classmates were taught what he thought was
a fantastic song with the mountain in it. He loved both
the song and the teacher of songs.

Lukingi lwefwe luno lwe Masaaba
This mountain of ours Mount Elgon
Lulimwo bihanwa bye kamakanga naabi –
Has in it many wondrous gifts
Mulimwo bisaali bibalaayi
In there are measureless forests
Mwabamwo tsimongwa;
In there are tall cliffs;
Mulimwo kamalea nabunulu
In there are sweet bamboo shoots
Mwabamwo tsimbama tsindakhani
In there are rare yams

Masaaba, Masaaba, Masaaba!
Mount Elgon, Mount Elgon, Mount Elgon!
Lukingi lwefwe luno lwe Masaaba
This mountain of ours Mount Elgon
Lulimwo bihanwa bye kamakanga naabi –
Has in it many wondrous gifts
Mulimwo Lulutsi Manafwa
In there is River Manafwa
Mwabamwo Lulutsi Solokho;
In there is River Solokho;
Mulimwo isonja
In there is circumcision dance
Mwabamwo inyembe
In there is circumcision knife

Masaaba, Masaaba, Masaaba...
Mount Elgon, Mount Elgon, Mount Elgon...

*   *   *

When Mwambu finally fell asleep, his spirit remained by the fireside of his childhood years, with his father and mother asking and answering riddle after riddle, and he wishing he could also pose a difficult riddle to which only he knows the clever answer, so that he could be given Masaaba's Mountain to eat...

*   *   *

Surrounded by his cheering campaign team, Mwambu delivered a rousing speech at the scheduled Elgonton South rally. To begin with, he thanked the immediate community of Elgonton South as well as the entire population of Elgonton District for having nurtured him by providing the cultural and social atmosphere under which he was privileged to have received quality education from primary school through university, thereby becoming the very first university graduate from the Elgonton region. Next he expressed special gratitude to the District Council, formerly the District Committee, for having provided a bursary that saw him through all his five years at the university, a bursary that came from the taxes paid by cotton and coffee growers all over the Elgonton region.

He went on to say that his pink-red man's education had not succeeded in brainwashing him into becoming the colonialist's tail-wagging dog. He assured the audience that, on the contrary, that education had only strengthened his resolve to be himself – an indigenous African – and to champion the right of all Elgonians and all the people of Uganda to determine their self-image and political destiny.

As he stood there on the dais of wooden planks, high above the throng, speaking of individual and collective human dignity and freedom from all fear and deprivation in Uganda and all over Africa in the coming decades, he experienced in his innermost self, a welling up of a sense of extreme personal satisfaction at the thought of his playing some top public role in championing the power of the people, and – as the pioneer solver of the trickiest community riddles – receiving, eating, and internalising, as his splendid reward, the very essence of whatever it is that the majestic Mountain of Masaaba encompasses in its height, breadth, depth, incomprehensiveness, and awesomeness.

'It's therefore as a mark of how much I appreciate you and owe to you,' he declared, 'that I would like to represent Elgonton South in Uganda's first parliament. If you vote me as your legislator, I pledge to tirelessly –'

'But before you pledge any lies,' shouted a drunken heckler from the crowd, 'I understand that your name is Abraham. Are you a Jew or a Moslem?'

'I'm neither of those!' Mwambu replied instantly, somewhat taken aback but keeping his cool. 'Abraham is just my Christian name.'

'So you're a Christian,' the heckler shot back, 'not an African!'

'I am an African, who is a Christian,' Mwambu countered. 'And I mean that; I am not a Christian who happens to be an African. I am an African first, by birth and upbringing; then Christian by much later adoption, into the universal family of all believers the one and only God the Creator and Redeemer.

'There you fail the test,' pronounced the heckler, giving his fellow heckler a nudge in the ribs. 'You've said that you're not a home-born African, but an imported one! You're like the Europeans who dwell in expensive quarters in Elgonton, and the Asians who live in middle-grade Indian quarters. You're not one to live with us black natives in bottom-grade, one-room black holes of Namakwekwe and Maluku!'

'But apart from that,' butted in the second pre-arranged heckler, 'in what year were you eaten by the knife?'

'Nineteen hundred fifty,' was the ready answer.

'And, if you've not read too many books, what's the name of that circumcision year?'

'Kwa Kamburikyi – it's known as Cambridge.'

'And can you also give us the names of five of your *bamakooki*, your circumcision-mates who are at present –'

'Enough of your questions!' shouted Mwambu's campaign manager, jumping to his feet. 'This is a political rally, not a drinking, *ndoleleele* pot!'

'Thank you, compatriot, for your timely intervention,' Mwambu said to his manager. 'But I was taking those interjections from the two gentlemen as part of their human rights, as part of their entitlement to the freedom of assembly and speech that I pledge to defend in parliament. And with that, I must say that the agenda of this rally has been accomplished. I have completed what I had to say this crucial afternoon. My last word is by way of repeating what I have already asked all Elgonians of Elgonton South to do, which is to vote massively for me by voting UDC!'

'Elgonton oyee!' shouted Mwambu's campaign manager, once more springing to his feet.

'Oyee!' replied the crowd with open hands raised towards the mountain.

'Elgonton South oyee!'

'Oyee!'

'UDC oyee!'

'Oyee!'

'Uganda oyee!'

'Oyee!'

'Mwambu oyee!'

'Oyee!'

When the noise and cheering of the excited crowd was dying down, the first drunken heckler yelled at the top of his hoarse voice, 'All right Mistah Mwambu, go your way but we have not yet talked our last with you!'

'Oyee!' yelled the second heckler in apparent agreement.

*   *   *

The first item of the 10.00 o'clock English news bulletin on Radio Uganda that same evening ran as follows:

'The chief editor of *The People's Herald*, Abraham Mwambu, was this evening assaulted and seriously injured by thugs at a place called Bumageni, some three miles outside Elgonton on the Elgonton-Tororo road.

'This occurred at about 7.30 p.m. The thugs, wearing hoods to disguise their identities, had erected a bogus temporary road-block by placing a huge log of wood across the road. They dragged all four occupants out of Mwambu's car; and while holding the other three at gun-point, severely beat up Mwambu. They stripped him naked, inflicted wounds on his head and his private parts, and then disappeared into the nearby eucalyptus forest at the approach of the next vehicle. The vehicle turned out to be a police patrol car. But by the time the police turned up, Mwambu had lost consciousness due to the bleeding. He was rushed to Elgonton Hospital, where he's still lying in critical condition.

'The police later apprehended three of the suspected culprits, and are holding them in protective custody at Elgonton Central Police Station.

'According to the three other occupants of Mwambu's car, the four occupants were returning from a political rally in Elgonton South constituency. Mwambu, the founder and current chief editor of *The People's Herald*, is standing as a UDC candidate. The nominations are scheduled for tomorrow, and candidates are required to be present in person at the nomination centres. There is no legal provision for nomination by proxy.

'This news bulletin comes to you in the Home Service of Radio Uganda.'

XX
In Debt to the People

'Father, have you heard the terrible news about Mwambu?' Mwambu's sister Khalayi asked, crashing through the open front door of her parents' house.

'Yes, my child,' he replied broken-heartedly. 'Buwayilila is home from Kampala on vacation: he knocked on the door before the stirring of the birds in their nests and told your mother and me that he had heard it on his father Kuloba's radio.'

'So Kuloba already knows.'

'Maybe he does, but I hear he didn't return last night from the political gathering that took place yesterday.'

'Somehow, he must have heard by now, father.'

'I don't care,' Masaaba bitterly replied, 'whether he has heard or not. This is my personal agony, not Kuloba's. I'm so angry for you, Mwambu my only son. And I know this trouble must be the work of evil neighbours who don't like you, who don't like me. It must be the vile deed of workers of witchcraft like Wopata my foul and envious *makooki*. It must be the work of Wopata and other neighbours with malice and wickedness in their hearts. But we shall find them. I shall find them, my daughter. I shall find them, and pay them back!'

'But for now, father, let's get ready to travel to Elgonton to see Mwambu.'

'Yes, my daughter, let's do that. Your mother should come with us, and yet one of us should stay behind to take care of the home. Let me figure out. I or your mother should at once travel with you.'

*   *   *

'My fellow woman,' said Wopata's wife to NaBusuulwa, 'what a great pity about your son!'

And she was thinking sadly about how her own son Wabwire had many seasons ago been shamefully circumcised while being forcibly held down on his back by the cruel hands of non-kinsmen.

'What a great pity, did you say?' NaBusuulwa angrily fired back. 'Some women have just gone past here laughing their way down the hill. You laugh your way up the hill!'

'Am I laughing, you wife of Masaaba?' Wopata's wife asked, feeling extremely hurt.

'Yes, you're laughing!'

'I came to express my sympathy, not to laugh.'

'Go express it at your own home! Sympathies are expressed about the dead, not about those who have been battered by envious wizards. Don't mock me to my face, you ugly witch! Go, go!'

Back in her own homestead, Wopata's wife vented to her husband her disgust with NaBusuulwa. 'That woman of Masaaba's – how could she shout at me like that! Is she the only woman whose son has come to grief? What sorrow have I not known? What sorrow?'

'Don't fret, woman,' Wopata consoled her. 'Their turn has come. That Masaaba, the wicked *makooki* that he is, cursed my son Wabwire and transformed him into the woman that he became. And now his only son has run into the trap of other doers of wickedness. Bu ho, ho! As the saying goes, "Does the child of a heartless butcher feel pain?" '

* * *

Back in Kampala, Nakintu was still awake and listening to the radio by 10.00 p.m. when her ears caught the shocking news about Mwambu. After an agonising, sleepless and endless night, she took the 6.00 a.m. Kampala-Elgonton bus.

On arrival in Elgonton she frantically rushed to the hospital. There she was told that Mwambu was not in the VIP wing but in the Intensive Care Unit, to which she was strictly denied admittance. Her pleas that she was the wife of the patient, and a nursing officer herself, fell on the deaf ears of the sister on duty. The sister explained that the patient was critically ill and had not yet regained consciousness. She also said that the patient had had the wound on his private organ immediately attended to but was still awaiting surgery for the severe injury he had incurred upon his head.

'A head injury is too bad!' Nakintu fumed. 'But why attack his private organ also? Why and how?'

'I have no answer to that one,' the sister clinically replied.

Appalled, Nakintu turned away and moved like a zombie through the streets of Elgonton to go find the resident Crown counsel to sound his opinion about the legal implications of the assault upon her husband.

* * *

The following day in the afternoon, the three suspects were duly produced before the District magistrate. Handcuffed and bare-footed, they were fixed in the docks, one after another, and made to swear upon the Bible or with the right hand over the heart, repeating after the court clerk that they were going to tell the whole truth and nothing but the truth, and so help them God!

The Crown counsel, a pioneer lawyer from neighbouring Teso, through an interpreter framed the charge of the Crown government against the accused, namely, that on the previous day at about 7.30 pm. at a place called Bumageni on the outskirts of the town, the three of them, together with their as yet un-apprehended accomplices, had without provocation and as a climax of an apparently premeditated scheme violently attacked and caused grave injury to one Mr. Abraham Mwambu with the intention of inflicting bodily harm on his person, as a consequence of which their victim was at that material time still lying in critical condition at the District hospital.

Presiding over the case was Mr. Dennis Bolton, an elderly and well-groomed English gentleman who had outstayed four of Her Majesty's Protectorate Governors in Uganda. From the ground rock of his being, he championed the civilizing mission of Great Britain to the benighted peoples of the world, and especially those of Africa, always maintaining his distance for fear of adulterating his speech and blackening his morals, always speaking to natives – whether job-hunters, civil servants or criminals – through an interpreter, and never demeaning himself to so much as learn one word of Africa's languages.

Mr. Bolton's court interpreter, Joseph Malemba, his hair beginning to turn grey at the edges, had been an interpreter for so long that it was difficult to think of the court furniture without him.

Taking over from the Crown counsel, Mr. Bolton asked the accused if they pleaded guilty or not guilty.

'Did you do bad,' Malemba interpreted, 'or did you do good?'

'We did not do bad,' they chorused.

'Accused Number One,' Mr. Bolton called out, 'what's your name, your address, and your station in life?'

'Iwe misitah,' Malemba started to interpret but was interrupted by the respondent.

'Ayi kani hiya ze wayiti maani wizautu yowa iyaasi andah maufu,' he said. 'Sah, yuu sipikyi tuu mi mayiselefu ini Ingilisi pulisi.'

'I'll sure do that!' answered Mr. Bolton. 'You speak English quite well;' he bitingly added, 'like the average educated Ugandan. Answer my question then. What is your name, your address and your work?'

'Mayi nemu isi Misitah Pitah Wayelo. Ayi havu bini e kyilakah ata Manafwa Kaunte hedikwotasi.

'What do you mean,' Mr. Bolton queried, 'by saying that you have been? What are you at present?'

'Fromu yesitade, sah,' Wayelo proudly revealed, 'ayamu kandideti fo Palyamenti.'

'Oh really?' Mr. Bolton asked, his eyes dilating in amazement.

'Yessah,' Wayelo confirmed with a satisfied smile.

'Do you know Mr. Abraham Mwambu, the victim of the attack under investigation?'

'Yessah. Wi weya ini ze semu kyilasi puraimare wanu ata Namwombe Puraimare Sikuulu.'

'And what's your basic education?'

'Mayi whati edukesoni, sah?'

'I said your *basic* education. In what class did you stop?'

Ini puraimare faivu, sah. Andah theya sikuulu fiisi bikcmu finisiti.'

'Andah zeya sikuulu fiisi bikemu finisiti,' Mr. Bolton mimicked.

'Yessah,' re-affirmed Wayelo.

'Aha,' sighed Mr. Bolton.

'And you accused Number Two,' Mr. Bolton continued, 'what is your name, your address, and your station in life?'

'You old one,' Malemba interpreted, 'the red one wants to know what they call you, where your house is located, and how you get your food.'

'I'm called Butoto from BuMutoto, and I get my food through being a circumciser. I'm a transformer of boys into men, of lovers into husbands, of the timid into valiant warriors, by virtue of my man-making, sharp-edged knife – that purifies through pain, that beautifies by imprinting the scar of manhood upon the paternal instrument of pleasure and procreation –'

'What a breathless mouthful that sounds to be!' impatiently remarked Mr. Bolton. 'Tell him to stop his gibberish nonsense; and require him to answer the question that was put to him.'

'He has actually answered it, Your Honour,' replied Malemba. 'He says that his name is Butoto from BuMutoto, by profession a circumciser.'

'By profession a circumciser, did you say?' Mr. Bolton could have spat on the floor to express his revulsion to the apparent blood-letting being probed. 'Does he know what *profession* means? Ask him that. And ask him about his education. What's his education?'

'Old one, where did you go,' Malemba asked, 'to read the alphabet?'

'*Nabirayo bwelabuule*,' Butoto proudly professed in the mother tongue.

'Sir,' Malemba interpreted for Mr. Bolton, 'he says that he walked past school when it was already dark.'

'And what does he mean by that? Mr. Bolton demanded.

'Sir,' Malemba simplified, 'he means that he has never been to school.'

'I thought as much!' pronounced Mr. Bolton. 'Let's turn to accused Number Three.'

The third suspect informed the court that his name was Musoola; that he came from the same village as Butoto; and that he was a casual labourer, an honest worker who earned his food by sweating for it along town pavements.

'How did you come to be part of this gang of thugs,' the Crown counsel asked him, 'that attacked the victim?'

'I was paid by people who said they needed some strong men to carry a heavy log of wood for a road-block to be mounted by Government officers to catch a certain dangerous criminal.'

Back to Butoto, Mr. Bolton asked him why, as a so-called circumciser, he came to be involved in the alleged vicious attack on the defendant.

'Exactly because I am a circumciser, that's why,' Butoto proudly replied.

'Will you talk sense?' the Crown counsel demanded.

'That's what I'm doing! The organisers of what happened had earlier asked me to join them to examine what Mwambu carries under his trousers, to determine whether he was a true man or not, if he had fully paid his debt to the people. Because if he had not paid that debt in full, he would be unfit to speak in the name of the real men in what they are calling the Big House of the People.'

'What does he mean,' Mr. Bolton sneered, 'by *a true man*? Malemba, ask him that.'

'What I mean to say,' Butoto replied, 'Is that I was to confirm whether Mwambu had been correctly circumcised or not.'

'And what do you mean by *correctly circumcised*?'

'You see, sir, we Elgonians are not Moslems or Jews.'

'That's obvious! So how different are you?'

'Sir, the Moslems cut off only the foreskin; and so do the Jews, I hear.'

'And you, what do you cut off?'

'We don't cut off only the foreskin. We also trim off a further round of skin higher up the male instrument. In this way we maximise the pain of true manhood, thereby creating a scar after the initiate has healed. That scar, sir, was missing on Mwambu's organ, as he had had a pink-red man's circumcision in a hospital. And that's why I was intending to cut off the excess skin on that organ of his which would turn into such a scar. Because for us, sir, that scar is everything. It's our badge of manhood.'

By the time Butoto was through with his reply, both Magistrate Bolton and Crown counsel were shaking their heads at the circumciser's evident conviction about his manhood notion.

'But if it was a scar,' Mr. Bolton asked Butoto, 'that you were looking for, how and why did you end up inflicting a wound on the victim's head as well?

'Sir, we were only intending to circumcise him properly,' Mutoto countered, 'but we were suddenly interrupted by your policemen!'

'Let me put it differently to you,' Mr. Bolton sardonically continued. 'Did you imagine that what you call his male instrument was partly located in his head?'

For the first time Butoto did not have a ready rejoinder.

*   *   *

The rest of the afternoon's court proceedings included interrogation of the three Crown witnesses who were with Mwambu in his car at the time of the assault. One of them asserted that he had recognised two of the hooded attackers who had held them at gun-point, and who were among those who had managed to escape. He identified one of them as being John Wambooza, the UDC chief mobiliser for Elgonton North. And he identified the second one as being Patrick Kuloba, an elder cousin to Mwambu.

*   *   *

Before adjourning the court, Mr. Bolton ruled that the accused three be returned to police custody and be produced again the following morning for judgement.

*   *   *

That very evening Wambooza and Kuloba were netted consuming mugs of crude *waragi* in a suburb of Elgonton, and they were duly produced in court the following day. They pleaded innocent to the charges of premeditated infliction of bodily harm to the person of the victim. Revealing that they and Mwambu were members of the same political party, they asked Mr. Bolton how they could do such a murderous thing to him.

Passing judgement, Mr. Bolton found both Wambooza and Kuloba, together with the three suspects of the previous day, to be guilty of the stated crime. They were each sentenced to twelve strokes of the buffalo whip, as well as a cash fine equivalent to one bull from each of them. The fine was to be paid to Mwambu to help offset some of the inconveniences resulting from the assault on him.

XXI
Because the World is Round

That same day, for hours on end Nakintu sat by her husband where he lay in bed in the hospital side-room. Wife-mother-nurse, anxious and waiting, she became what wives become when some random calamity or some natural infirmity breaks their men and turns them into infants again. It could be a fractured spine or a swollen spleen. And then the men-infants shamelessly have their soiled pants and towels changed for them, their urine collected into bed-side potties and taken away by their wife-mother-nurses. In that ultimate helplessness, even the former perennial bully may be pierced to the core by the all-caring tenderness of the wife who was never before thanked even once in a life of full-time burden-bearing and scrubbing.

*   *   *

In the afternoon of the second full day in hospital, Mwambu started slowly coming to. Early the previous evening the senior neuro-surgeon had removed a small blood clot from his brain.

Oh, Dr. Kiryabwire had magic hands and a compassionate heart! When your loved one had been involved in some terrible tragedy, and he was being wheeled into the operating theatre, and only those masked junior doctors were working on him – you would pace the corridor with increasing heaviness in your breast. But if your beloved was being taken to the theatre and Dr. Kiryabwire came along on his way to carrying out yet another of his deft operations, he would stop by you and greet you with eyes that understood your agony before proceeding to his task – and you would pace the corridor with rising hope in your breast.

* * *

Opening his eyes on his wife, Mwambu dreamily called out, 'Mayi...Mummy...Mother mine...Or are you Khalayi...? Child of my mother....Mummy...Mother mine...'

'I'm Sarah,' Nakintu said, holding his hand tenderly, caressingly, and blowing her warm breath on it. 'I'm Sarah...your wife....Yes, your wife....not mother...No, not mother... Do you hear me, Mwambu darling? You'll be all right. You've been unwell but you're getting better... You're out of danger now...'

'Ah, you're...Na-kintu....Na-ki-thing...Femal-thinammy ....Female-thing...a...ma...bob....'

'Yes, darling, I'm your Sarah, and you're my Abraham,' she said with a nod and a smile.

'And how are you?'

'I'm quite fine.'

'How is my mother?'

'She too is quite fine.'

'How is my father?'

'He too is – '

But he did not hear her answer, his mind abruptly distracted by his strange surroundings: grey curtains, grey bedside wash-stand, grey towel, grey ceiling, grey –

'And where am I?' he yelled, taking fright. 'Where am I, and what happened to me? Sa-----rah!'

'You're with me here,' Nakintu said, trying to sound as casual as she could muster, 'in hospital.'

Like lightning, the facts of what had been done to him broke upon him. He quickly sat up in a panic, threw off the bed-sheet down to his knees, made a guess at the pain between his legs, and then as quickly fell back mumbling and covered his face with the bed-sheet.

Oh hell my God the bastards my People's Herald going to heaven lying on my back the thugs my people Sarah my mother my father me I myself what is a man a human being with tail in front of so much fuss makes the world go round makes the prostitutes go round pimps and popes with or without foreskin like cats monkeys dogs he-goats and snakes shading their slough chameleons their molt but no self pity I must face it like a man like who like who like who...

'Mwambu darling,' Nakintu called softly, removing the bed-sheet from his face and tenderly stroking his forehead with her hands. 'Abby my darling, you were talking in your half-sleep. Please don't.'

'I please don't what? I mean, was I sleeping or talking?'

He opened his eyes.

'Yes, I think I was dreaming...of those years, of those yarns, of those yearnings...of those hopes...of childhood by the mountain... of the child and the drums...of the child and the man... of the child and the beasts. Of the child and the human beasts, beasts, beasts –'

'Please Abby,' Nakintu tenderly interrupted, 'you must not say such fanciful things.'

'Did you say,' he asked, suspiciously surveying the room, 'that I'm in my bed? Is it the bed in the village or in Kampala?'

'No, darling, it's a different bed.'

'But I know this room, these windows, and this door – where am I?'

'No, Mwambu darling, you don't know this room.'

As tactfully and as slowly as she could, Nakintu explained the events of the last three days, right from the point Mwambu and his colleagues in ran into the ambush of his attackers. Without naming the suspects, she mentioned the arrest of some of his suspected attackers.

'The devilish attack was by my political opponents,' Mwambu firmly announced. 'But why does it look like I've been here before? Why and how?'

'No, Mwambu, you haven't been here before! It must be what is called *déjà vu*. It's the odd feeling or sensation that one seems to be remembering a scene one has never seen before or –'

'No, no, Sarah!' he countered as he tried to sit up, looking wildly about him. 'This is *no* déjà vu! Where did you say we are?'

'We're in Elgonton town,' she replied, gently pulling him down onto his back.

'And which particular place in Elgonton town is this?'

'It's Elgonton Hospital.'

'My God, my God!' Mwambu exclaimed, his lower jaw unhinging. 'I told you so, Sarah! How we end up where we started! This definitely proves that the world is round.'

'Oh, does it?' She was in panic – was he mentally relapsing?

'Yes, it does. Twelve years ago, this is exactly where I was circumcised.'

'Oh, don't say!' Nakintu exclaimed.

'Yes! This next room must be the operating theatre.'

'That's right. It's where you had the surgery last night.'

'And this must be the very room where I waited after my circumcision for the school bus to pick me and take me back to Elgonton Secondary School.'

Nakintu was at a loss about what to say next.

'But, darling,' she ventured, 'don't think too much about what those thugs tried to do to you.'

'What exactly did the thugs try to do to me?'

'Oh, don't worry. I've told you three of them were arrested. They're bound to pay heavily following their appearance in court yesterday.'

Mwambu was so terrified he nearly jumped out of bed.

'You mean,' he fumbled, gripping her right hand and staring into her eyes, 'that the incident has been made public?

'No, I don't mean that. As a matter of fact, the court is completely on your side.'

'Oh no!' Mwambu groaned. 'Sarah, did you take the matter to court?'

'No, Abby, I've done no such thing. And I should tell you that I have received many expressions of   support since the evening of the barbaric attack on you. Not only were the damned rogues condemned in the strongest terms on radio...'

'On radio!' He shot out of bed.

'On radio did you say?' He gripped Nakintu by both shoulders and looked wildly about the room.

And she was frightened of him in real earnest.

'Tell me, Sarah,' he exhaled, 'did you make a radio announcement?'

'Oh no, no, no!' She was glad she had merely been misunderstood. 'Abby, it was not an announcement. It was a news item on the radio, and I had nothing to do with its being aired. In fact, it was through hearing the radio bulletin that I myself came to learn about the attack and rushed to come and be with you.'

'My God, my God!' He walked about the room. 'My God, my God!' He slumped on the bed upon his back, closed his eyes, and watched upon an invisible ceiling a phantasmagorical filmstrip of his soul – distant past, recent and present.

XXII
Shadows from the Back of the Head

Hours later Mwambu's memory had erased most of what had passed between him and Nakintu after he partially regained consciousness. The nurse on duty knocked on the door and announced that the patient's mother was outside. After checking Mwambu's condition a little, she decided that he was stable enough to receive his mother. She let NaBusuulwa in, stepped into the corridor, and closed the door behind her.

'Oh my child, I'm so happy to see you alive!' NaBusuulwa cried, bursting into tears as she knelt by Mwambu's bed. 'And you my daughter,' she said to Nakintu, 'what a terrible experience for you!'

'Good to see you, mother,' smiled Mwambu.

'And it has been very hard for you too, mother,' Nakintu added. 'For two days neither of us could be allowed in to see him.'

'Yes, yes! But today the nurse says even his father and sister can be let in. They're in town and on their way here. She says they can come in when I go out, so that there aren't too many visitors at a time.'

'That's good,' remarked Nakintu. 'He's still very weak.'

'But those murderers,' NaBusuulwa fumed, 'how could they want to kill my child? Mwambu, why would that Wayelo of Namisindwa want to kill you?'

'Was Wayelo one of them, mother?' Mwambu asked, musingly screwing up his eyes.

'Yes, he was! And there were two others in court. One of them claimed to be a circumciser, but he must be a cut-throat who was looking for human blood to drink!'

'They're terrible vultures and ogres!' Nakintu angrily butted in.

'But worst of all, Mwambu,' NaBusuulwa raged on, unaware of what was going on in Elgonton court that day, 'is that there's talk that Kuloba was one of your attackers.'

'What!' exclaimed Nakintu.'

'Our very Patrick Kuloba,' Mwambu incredulously asked, raising himself upon his elbows, 'was one of my attackers... mother, is that what you're saying?'

'That's what we hear from those who were in court yesterday. They say he escaped after the attack on you, thinking nobody had recognized him. But they're hunting for him, and he hasn't been at home since the day of the ambush.'

Nakintu could make no sense of it. 'Wonders never cease, they say,' she sighed. 'Is it Kuloba the father of Buwayilila, and Mwambu's elder first cousin, that you're talking about?'

'Yes, that's the very Kuloba,' NaBusuulwa confirmed. 'But, children,' she said after a lengthy pause, 'maybe I shouldn't sound so mad. Maybe I need to explain something.'

'And what could that be, mother?' Mwambu asked interestedly.

NaBusuulwa, who had been kneeling before Mwambu's bed all this time, sat herself on the floor and stretched her legs.

'You see, that Kuloba bears Masaaba and you a grudge, from before you were born.'

'What!' Mwambu was both shocked and intrigued, while Nakintu tried her best to follow the general drift of the conversation in a language she didn't understand very well.

'Yes, he does. For one thing, he thinks that he's your father.'

'I beg your pardon!' Mwambu instantly shot up and sat rigidly on the bed as he blinked several times in disbelief.

'Go on, mother! What's all this?'

'Well, as I've said, the grudge begins before you were born. When your father Masaaba married me I was still very young. How many years old was I? I was as many years as there are fingers on both hands and toes on one foot. Masaaba was as many as there are fingers on both hands and toes on both feet, plus the fingers of one more hand. And Kuloba was as many as there are fingers on both hands and toes on both feet. So you can see that Masaaba was older than Kuloba by the fingers of one hand; and Kuloba was older than me by the same fingers of one hand,'

'Mother is saying,' Mwambu simplified for Nakintu, 'that she married at the age of fifteen; when Masaaba my father-to-be was twenty-five, and Kuloba his nephew was twenty.'

'Both men,' NaBusuulwa continued, 'had been courting me. But I kept my purity. When I got married to Masaaba, Kuloba could hardly bear the thought of losing me to his uncle. He was consumed with anger and jealousy. One day, within the first two moons of my becoming Masaaba's wife, I was returning from the well past Kuloba's house after sunset. I coughed and announced who I was to assure his household that it was just me going by. I didn't know that he was alone in the house. He followed me. He asked me to put down my water-pot and talk with him a little. I refused. Acting like a madman, he forcefully put down my water-pot and wanted to lie with me against my wish. When I tried to scream, he slapped his hand upon my mouth and threatened to strangle me. He then raped me.'

'Oh, no, he didn't!' Mwambu yelled, as his incredulous eyes met with Nakintu's frightened ones. 'Sarah, mother is saying that while still a young bride, she was raped by Kuloba before I was born.'

'Yes, it's true, Mwambu my child,' his mother feebly assured him. 'I conceived inside that very moon. Of course I've never come near Kuloba again by myself, but every time he gets an evil chance he keeps on hinting that you Mwambu resemble him as if you were his son. But then, it's not surprising when clansmen resemble one another, since they come from one ancestor.'

'Mother,' Mwambu wearily said, 'you've told us enough, or more than enough! Has my father ever heard any of these ugly words of Kuloba?'

'Yes. Once when you were a baby, Kuloba got himself foolishly drunk and told Masaaba that he should not be so sure you were his son.'

'That would seem to explain a remark or two that my father has made in my hearing about what I should be if I'm his true son!'

'Yes. I myself twice heard those remarks.'

'And about Buwayilila – what has Kuloba, when once perhaps drunk, said about him?'

'Oh, he nearly beat his wife Mayuba to death, while she was still breast-feeding Buwayilila, when he came upon her singing the baby to sleep, and intoning that he should grow up to be tall and clever like you Mwambu.'

'He beat her up for wishing just that?'

'Yes. "Am I the father or Mwambu?" he roared at her.'

*But you know everything, O God...*Mwambu mused. 'And now, mother, let me ask you the question of a lifetime. And I'm sure you know the answer.' He took a deep breath. 'According to you, who is my father?'

In turn, NaBusuulwa took a deep breath followed by a troubled sigh.

'To tell you the utter truth, my son, I don't know who your father is!'

Mwambu was aghast and speechless. *My mother doesn't know who my father is...! That means I'm Kuloba's son, doesn't it...? And if so, then not only is Buwayilila my son; he's Kuloba's grandson...! And Mayuba wife of Kuloba made me, when she raped me, master of her bed alongside Kuloba...and therefore a bed-competitor of my cousin-father...!*

'Sarah,' he called, as a strange feeling of relief swept through him, 'what mother has just been saying encourages me to say what I'm going to say. It has seemed like a sensitive secret up until now, and it certainly doesn't deserve to be kept as such.'

'Then out with it!' Nakintu prompted him.

'Buwayilila is not my nephew. He's my son.'

Nakintu's face went blank. *Just the one thing that never occurred to me...never...and Mwambu has kept it this long...as long as I've kept mine...it's like a vengeance... this incredible coincidence, you ancestors of mine...*

'Won't you say something?' Mwambu plainly asked Nakintu.

'Ye-ye-yes, I will.'

'Are you too disappointed in me, Sarah?' he asked with a remote stare, as if he was making out something on the mind's horizon.

'No, it's not that,' she sighed. 'It's that I have something as grave to tell, but can't yet bring myself to do so.'

'Nothing can be as grave as what I've heard today.'

'Please don't press me.'

'No, I dare not press you. But today appears to be the day of our release, the day of our salvation. Whatever it is, my heart will take it, embrace it, and bear it for the love of you. And, I must add, for God's sake. Get it off your mind, forever; and you'll become new, and feel new!'

Nakintu buried her face into the blanket on Mwambu's bed and burst into tears.

'Sarah my darling one,' Mwambu whispered in a tone of ultra tenderness, 'get it off your mind!'

'Nantongo isn't my cousin or niece,' she announced with a deep groan.

'What do you mean by that?' Mwambu cut in, visibly puzzled.

'She's my daughter,' Nakintu let out.

Mwambu's mouth fell open, while Nakintu resumed her flow of tears. *But, Mwambu, you must have long known this...from some mysterious intelligence of yours... you often came so close to telling me you knew all about it ...*

Mwambu broke the lengthy silence with a startling laugh, enigmatic in its import. *And so Buwayilila and Nantongo playing teenage sex did so as step-brother and step-sister! What a damned world!*

'Mother,' he said, drawing NaBusuulwa into the conversation, 'I know you've not followed the last part of the conversation between your daughter and me, as it was in a foreign language. But she and I have so much in common, so much to bind us with ropes of forgiveness and love – or ropes of vengeance and hatred.'

'That sounds good, my child. I mean the ropes of forgiveness and love.'

'Yes, mother. Still, she'll need time, and I'll need time to get to the bottom of what happened, and why it happened.' And he thought – *Like that virgin spot of blood on the white linen of our wedding night. How on earth does a mothering woman successfully trick a man into believing she is a virgin?*

'But now I must leave you, Mwambu my child. If I leave, then Khalayi and your father can be let in. And please remember that Masaaba is the father you know!'

'Yes, mother. But even as you go, ask yourself if your son's destiny now in any way depends on who fathered him – whether Masaaba or Kuloba.'

'Stay well, Mwambu,' NaBusuulwa said in a cheerless voice. 'And get out of here soon.'

'Go well, mother,' Mwambu blankly replied. 'And see you all before polling day.'

XXIII
And I Left Them There to Come
And Tell You

In response to the news of the serious attack on Mwambu on the eve of nominations, the National Electoral Committee of Uganda Democratic Congress had called an emergency meeting the following morning at which he was replaced as the party candidate for Elgonton South by his old schoolmate, Peter Wayelo. And it was Wayelo that met the qualifications for nomination as a Parliamentary candidate by the end of the morning that day. And it was he that won the Elgonton South seat in the elections, beating two college-educated rival candidates from other political parties.

*   *   *

Still at Elgonton Hospital by polling day, Mwambu had been advised by the senior surgeon to remain there for one more week under expert observation. So it was from hospital that he learnt of Wayelo's eleventh-hour candidacy and amazing victory in the national elections.

*   *   *

One week after the general elections, Mwambu was discharged from hospital, five days to the historic day of Uganda's Independence from Britain. Still smarting from having been out-played in the race for Parliament by what seemed the dirtiest political trickery imaginable, he resolved not to turn up for the Independence Day Celebrations at the magnificently constructed Kololo Stadium.

Instead, he set himself the task of being at the offices of *The People's Herald* across Independence night producing a Special Edition of the paper for the first day of Independence. To that Special Edition he would contribute a feature article on the country's political aspirations. He would entitle the article, "The Cost of Knowledge and Freedom".

Two days into writing his article, Mwambu was shocked to hear on a mid-day radio newscast the line-up of Hosea Hamilton Otebo's cabinet ministers in the imminent First Parliament of Uganda. Two names on the list made Mwambu sit up and shake his ears. One was that of the Member of Parliament for South Central constituency, Michael Musisi, appointed minister of Justice and Attorney General. And the other was that of Peter Wayelo, Member of Parliament for Elgonton South constituency, as the minister of Education.

'What!' Mwambu exploded in utter amazement. 'Musisi, M^2 college drop-out, shrine guardian, ancestral god – and now appointed a government minister in charge of Justice! And Peter Wayelo the murderous semi-illiterate is entrusted with the country's education from kindergarten to university!'

That propelled his mind to return in a creative craze to his article. With the types of Musisi and Wayelo making their ridiculous entrance onto the political stage – he decided that his article must raise an alarm over the tragic mismatch between culture, education and politics that the infant country appeared to be headed for.

But on the sunnier side of times still unborn, he was going to change the masthead and logo of *The People's Herald*. Since its inception, he reminded himself, the paper had had the cock as its symbol, typifying a new dawn for the struggling, enslaved people of Africa's heartland.

And now he got his brainwave. His new symbol for the next generation must be that of something that succeeds dawn, which supersedes the cock. And that something was surely the full round sun risen clear above the mountain – Mountain of the Sun...*and that is the mountain of my un-making and re-making ....mountain of my un-doing and re-doing...mountain of my childhood dreams and nightmares...mountain that I take and eat... mountain that eats me in return...and transforms me utterly, such that...*

Suddenly, his mind went off at a tangent –

From a certain chamber of his memory the Chancellor's send-off remarks on graduation day provocatively resounded in his inner ears...*This is your day of commissioning...we have provided you with dynamic packages of knowledge and professional kits... to go and cause a revolution wherever you find yourselves... to push back the boundaries of darkness...I'm depending on you... not to betray the confidence I have placed in you...*

Then, as he was writing the concluding sentence of his newspaper article, from deep down in his interior the taunting, menacing words of the two drunken hecklers at his very last political rally came suddenly spouting to the surface. *Can you also give us the names of five of your bamakooki, your circumcision-mates...I understand that your name is Abraham, are you a Jew or a Moslem? All right Mistah Mwambu, go your way – but we have not yet talked our last with you...*

'And for sure,' he vocally admitted to himself, 'they meant what they said. And they came for me. But neither am I through with them. With this article, my campaign against the blind enemies of true culture, the intellect and the spirit has barely begun...or what other weapons might one need...?'

* * *

And I, Nalukano son of story-tellers of olden times, left those people there in that strange land to come and tell you what happened.

Pthow! Story, remain a dwarf while I grow!
Pthow! Story, remain a dwarf while my listeners grow!
Pthow! Story, remain a dwarf while my readers grow!